Gunshy, the new Jen Pierce Mystery
by Sharon Lee

Having survived a run-in with a killer as well as a not-quite accident that destroyed her prized Camaro and almost cost her her life, Baltimore-transplant Jen Pierce has settled into her new role as a respected small-town journalist in Wimsy, Maine.

That role includes certain social obligations. She's always going to have a seat at a town meeting, just *has* to catch the school's anti-drug play, and as winter comes on there's always something else surprising needing to be done.

This year's first surprise is who's throwing that must-do pre-Yule party. And the second is who she meets there.

GUNSHY

SHARON LEE

SRM Publisher, Ltd.
Unity, ME

Gunshy Copyright © 2006 by Sharon Lee

Gunshy

Published by SRM Publisher Ltd..
PO Box 179
Unity, ME   04988

Editing by Steve Miller
Copyediting by Elektra Hammond
Interior layout by Steve Miller

Cover design by Richard Horn

ISBN 0-9776639-2-2

http://www.srmpublisher.com
First SRM Publisher edition: August 2006

Printed in the United States of America
0 9 8 7 6 5 4 3 2 1

For Vicki Brown

Special thanks to Chick Love for his help with police procedures. Any errors are my own.

1989

Central Maine

GUNSHY

1

The radio was playing "Winter Wonderland" when I blew into Mainely Manes. The wind and I tussled for the door, which contest of brute strength I won, but not easily.

"Brr!" I told Stacy the receptionist, and she nodded, screwing her tiny face up into an eloquent grimace of distaste. I sighed and went to hang up my parka.

"Winter Wonderland" burbled merrily on and I wondered, as I struggled with the parka's zipper, if it had been written by a Floridian, a Californian or a citizen of the southwestern desert. Clearly, it couldn't have been written by anyone who had actually experienced winter, Maine-style.

"Is it really only December seventh?" I demanded, crossing the room to Philip's station.

"It gets worse before it gets better, darling." He shook the apron out with a magician's swirl and fastened it around my neck while I held my hair high. "You ought to be used to this by now," he said, coming around to the counter for his comb. "An old Mainer like you."

"Every Mainer I talk to hates winter," I told him. "The bangs need to be cut."

"Talk to the ice-fishing and snowmobile crowd," Philip recommended. Abruptly, he shook his head, put the comb down with a small, petulant click and stepped behind the chair. He used both hands to lift my hair and caught my eye in the mirror.

"You really ought to do something with this."

"I am doing something with it," I said. "I'm letting it grow."

"Don't be a bitch, darling." Philip said placidly. "Letting it grow was one of your better ideas—you're light-years ahead of that butch 'do you had when you hit town. Now we need to refine the look."

I eyed his reflection. "This sounds suspiciously like the sell for a fifty-dollar perm."

"Good God, do I look like a barbarian?" he demanded, stung to the core of his artistic soul. "What you absolutely do *not* need is more mass around that face!"

"I knew it was going to come down to my face," I said resignedly. "It always does. Forget the bangs, OK? I'll grow 'em to my knees."

Philip sighed and lowered my hair gently to my shoulders before coming around to the front of the chair. He leaned one hip against the counter and crossed his arms over his meager chest.

"It's not a bad face. In fact, it's rather–interesting. Thin and interesting. *Thin* is the operative word, darling. All those thick, luscious waves simply overpower you. It's time for A Look."

"It's time for my bangs to get cut," I told him. "And then it's time for me to finish the rest of my errands and go to work. I'm thirty-five years old–I don't need A Look, I need a retirement account."

Philip shook his head, shifted and reached for the comb and scissors. "Do me a favor, will you, Jen?" he asked, combing my bangs over my eyebrows.

I squinted my eyes shut. "What's that?"

"Don't tell anybody you get your hair cut here."

*

The wind blew me up and down Main Street, releasing and reclaiming me in turn at LaVerdiere's drug store, Dore's Hardware and Mother's Pantry. I tucked the last of my purchases into a canvas carryall, zipped the top and slung the thing over my shoulder before surrendering myself to the wind for the two block walk to the offices of the *Wimsy Voice*. I would be forty-five minutes ahead of my shift, but I would be out of the wind. If God and the ancient steam heat plant were good, I'd even be warm.

I crossed Main Street with the wind at my back and turned the corner into Preble just as a particularly playful gust descended.

The new wind snatched the bag on my shoulder, twisted it and jerked it to my elbow, at the same time flinging a scatter of gravel into my face. I swore, grabbed, then staggered as the wind whooshed around me like a pack of high-spirited puppies and roared off, abruptly abandoning me to gravity.

A hand caught my elbow, steadying me. City reflexes kicked in and I jerked back. The hand tightened slightly, keeping me on my feet. I shook the hair out of my face and the gravel out of my eyes, looked—and smiled.

"Fox."

"Jennifer," he returned seriously. "Nice day."

"I've seen nicer," I told him. He raised an eyebrow and released my elbow.

"Recently?"

I laughed. "Point."

He turned and walked with me down Preble, toward the river and the *Voice* building.

"Done shopping for the day?"

I nodded. "Heading for work, frigid but early. Murphy's Law dictates that the steam plant will either not be working at all or so well we'll have to open the windows, and that it won't matter anyhow, because Bill Jacques will send me out to do a man-on-the-street."

Fox smiled his slight smile. "That sounds remarkably like Bill," he agreed and tipped his head. "Are you early enough so you can stop for a cup of coffee?"

Michaelson's Gourmet Coffee Shop and Café was right across Preble Street, and a steaming cup of Swiss-chocolate-almond sounded like pure heaven. I smiled.

"Good idea."

*

We hung our jackets on pegs by the door and found a table in an alcove dominated by a large plant of the type known as "foliage". Micky Michaelson came bustling over, pad ready, smile on his mustached face.

"Mr. Foxwell," he said, nodding respectfully, as one does to summer people or other privileged classes. For me, it was a wider smile and a casual, "Hi, Jenny."

We ordered–hazelnut for Fox, Swiss-chocolate-almond for me–and Micky swooped away, returning in less than a minute with two thick white mugs, gently steaming, and a pitcher of honest-to-goodness cow's cream.

"Enjoy," he said, and left us to it.

I poured cream, stirred, and Fox did the same. Neither of us bothered with sugar.

Fox is David Foxwell, American citizen of various foreign parts, most lately out of Austin, Texas. He calls himself a computer geek, which is understatement. In the computer geek world, he's royalty: *Lord* Fox. In Wimsy, he runs a computer bulletin board called *Random Access*, which is where I met him. He's thirty-five years old, a widower, and he came to Maine to kill a man.

I wrapped my hands around the warm white mug and breathed in Swiss-chocolate-almond steam. "Yum," I said and sighed in bliss.

"Reconciled to winter now?" Fox murmured and I glanced over to him.

Fox looks more or less like his namesake–auburn hair and honey skin, long nose and pointed chin. His eyes are an extremely dark blue, black in dim lighting. He smiles, very slightly. I've yet to hear him laugh.

"You do not reconcile with a Maine winter, you grit your teeth and endure it," I told him. "If I didn't live here, I wouldn't."

He sipped his coffee, watching me over the mug's rim. "You could move back to Baltimore."

I shook my head. "I own that house on the Point. I'd have to sell to afford the move and the housing market in Maine doesn't exist–especially for beat-up old farmhouses and ten acres of overgrown field."

"So you're stuck."

I frowned, considering that while I sipped coffee.

"I don't think *stuck*," I said, slowly. "I don't think that. See, when Aunt Jen left me the house, I came up here with the intention of putting it right on the market. Take the money and run. Thought maybe I'd get enough for a down payment on one of those tiny row houses on Tyson Street–" Like Fox would know where Tyson Street was. I threw him an apologetic glance. "Right downtown," I explained. "Walking distance of the harbor and the music clubs, Lexington Market . . ."

He nodded. "But you didn't sell," he prompted. "Why not?"

I shrugged, feeling rather inadequate to the task of explaining Wimsy's lure.

"It was–quiet," I managed eventually. "I grew up in the suburbs–moved to the city at seventeen and never moved out. Three a.m., four–there's always some noise, somewhere. Traffic, sirens, radios, the conversation from the apartment next door . . . The first morning I woke up in that house–my house–you know what I heard?" I didn't wait for him to shake his head. "Birds. Not pigeons. Birds. I must've laid in bed an hour, listening to the birds sing." I shook my head.

"I don't like winter," I said, "but I can put up with it, for the rest of the year." I sipped coffee and glanced over. Fox was watching me with quiet attention, long fingers wrapped loosely 'round his mug.

"There's one thing I do like about the winter," I said. "When it gets cold enough–when ice is *in* as Harry says? You can walk right out on the Smoke–walk across to Waterville, if you want to." I hesitated, suddenly wondering . . .

"Are you leaving?" I blurted, because Fox's business was done and there was nothing to tie him here. Just because he'd hung around an extra couple months after Reverend Stern had reaped what he'd sown . . . "No reason for you to put up with a Wimsy winter. Just pack up your computers and head back to Texas."

"Texas does not lie particularly close to my heart," he said calmly. "And I don't think I've seen a real winter since we were in Germany, when I was fourteen." He finished his coffee and gave me one of his slight smiles. "I think I'd enjoy walking across the Smoke."

I returned the smile, then moved my eyes on the pretext of finishing my own coffee. Fox would be in Wimsy for the winter. It was ridiculous how happy that made me.

"When does your shift start?"

I put the mug down. "Six."

"Ah." He glanced down at his wrist. "Five-fifty-four."

"Time to move on." I reached for my pocketbook.

Fox waved a lazy hand. "I'll get it," he said, and was gone before I could protest.

Shaking my head, I wriggled out from beneath the foliage and retrieved my jacket from its peg. I was still struggling with the damned zipper when Fox reappeared and pulled on his own coat. *His* zipper went up in one effortless glide; he pulled the hood over his hair.

I finally conquered my zipper and pulled the parka's collar up in lieu of the hood I didn't have. Fox opened the door and we went out together, into a wind that seemed not as cold as it had been.

2

Maine has its share of odd town names—Mars Hill, Skowhegan, Argyle, Rosemary—and there's nothing all that odd about Wimsy, once you know it was called after Jebediah Wimsy, who settled the Point along about 1780.

Waterville is the nearest city, two miles from Wimsy Main Street, across the Big Smoke River. Next town beyond that is Winslow, across two more rivers—Sebasticook and Kennebec. Three or four miles south, where the Smoke gets swallowed by the Kennebec, is Twin Rivers State Park, at the Vassalboro town line.

Fox left me at the *Voice*'s front door. I crossed the tiny lobby and went up the fire stairs, ignoring the two-bit elevator. I hate elevators.

Bill Jacques nodded as I strode into the newsroom. "Ms. Pierce. Glad you could make it."

I resisted the temptation to stick my tongue out at him; settling instead for a frosty, "Good evening, Mr. Jacques," as I swept past on the way to third desk, my reportorial perch for the last twenty months.

Second desk is Sue Danforth, a pinch-faced woman who looks years older than the thirty-two life has handed her so far. She looked up with her version of a smile as I went past. "Good evening, Jennifer."

"Hi." I paused, smiling down into her tired blue eyes. "Working tonight?"

"Just finishing up," she said. "Pam's watching Molly, so I can be a couple minutes late."

Pam is Sue's sister; Molly is Sue's daughter. Molly's dad is Jimmy Danforth, who works in the woods when he's sober. Unfortunately, he's not sober all that often, and tends toward belligerence, drunk or not. He cost Sue a small fortune in bail, broken furniture and bruises before she finally got fed up, changed the locks and filed a protection order.

The last I'd heard, Jimmy was "on the town," as the phrase goes–getting food stamps and drunk more often than ever. His name was in the cop log every week or so: Disorderly conduct, driving while intoxicated, shoplifting–that one was cigarettes, mostly.

"I've got a call in to the state police," Sue said, easing back into her chair like she thought a sudden move would pain her. She reached for her notebook, flipped pages, and nodded.

"Hit and run out on the School Road–Angel Bolduc, sixteen–apparently hit while she was walking home from hockey practice, slid into the ditch. Guy in a truck happened to glance down, saw the red coat and got on the radio. The hospital's supposed to call, too, with an update." She glanced up at me. "The file name's *run*. Fill in the blanks for me and send it when it's ready?"

"Sure."

"Thanks," she said, and shook her head. "What kind of person do you have to be, to hit somebody like that and just drive away?"

"Maybe they didn't know," I offered half-heartedly. Sue snorted.

"They knew," she said darkly, and eased toward her screen. "I've got another couple 'graphs on this one . . ."

I took the hint and moved on to my desk, reached behind the old CPU and flicked up the switch, then went back to the cloakroom to struggle free of the parka.

The computer had loaded by the time I returned. The heading above the four-choice menu read **Karen's Computer**.

Karen Hopkins had been third-desk reporter before me. She'd fled back to her native California two years ago and I'd succeeded to her position a bare four months after her departure, but I'd never gotten around to changing the name on the menu. If asked, I would have said that the name over the menu was a matter of utter indifference to me.

This evening, finger poised over '1' for 'Write', I frowned at the menu head, unaccountably annoyed.

Really, Jennifer, how indolent can you be?

Before I finished chiding myself, my fingers had moved, dropping me into DOS and pulling up the .BAT file. It took approximately three seconds to find and alter the proper line, save the batch and reboot.

The computer groaned, struggled, beeped. The screen ghosted, then offered up the menu: *Jen's Computer* it announced. I nodded, absurdly pleased with myself, and hit '1' for 'Write'.

*

I've worked as a secretary, an advertising copywriter, a computer sales person, and a waitress in my time, but reporting takes the cake for sheer unstructured wackiness. You go out, you interview someone, you go in, you write, you go out for the cop log, you come back, you take a couple obits, make a few phone calls, check something in the story morgue, go out for another interview—or maybe a meeting—write, set up interviews for tomorrow or the next day, clarify points or rewrite to editorial direction, all the while keeping one ear on the scanner and writing like hell, especially if you're on late shift, because the deadline for all stories is 11 p.m., sharp.

The first couple weeks I worked at the *Voice*, I thought I was going to go crazy.

Then, I started to like it.

Now, I can't think of anything else I'd rather be doing as paying work.

Reporters carry a license to pry. Armed with only a pad, a Bic and a couple questions, I take on townspeople, police officers, shopkeepers, dissidents, selectpersons, school board officials and occasional bad asses. It's astonishing, the information people will happily give to "the press." All I have to do is–ask.

I've had assignments I haven't liked: Talking to the mother of a four-year-old drowning victim. Interviewing the old man whose equally old dog was shot dead in the dooryard by hunters who swore they'd thought the animal was a deer. Car crashes. . . I really don't like to cover car crashes.

Mostly, though–taken on average–I like my job. I like getting out and around and meeting the people in my new hometown. I like the weirdness, and the chaos. I like the way that a newspaper actually comes out of it all, three days a week, every week, regular as winter.

The phone rang. I cradled it between cheek and shoulder while I uncapped the Bic one-handed and flipped my pad to a clean sheet.

It was Second Selectman Lyle Saunders, calling to be sure I'd be at meeting this evening–selectperson's meeting, that would be, my every-other-Tuesday assignment.

"Be some interesting tonight," Lyle confided. "Comprehensive Plan Committee's going to present its recommendations."

"Hot stuff," I said, deadpan.

"That's all right." Lyle chuckled. "Be coffee, anyway, and a place in from the weather."

I grinned and put the Bic down. "You've convinced me. I'll see you there."

"Well, naturally," he said, and broke the connection.

"Mail for you, Jen." Carly the copy editor was standing at my right shoulder, fluttering a meager fan of number ten envelopes.

"Hey, thanks." I took them, then made a snatch as a shorter, classier envelope slid free, catching it before it hit the floor.

"What's this?" I asked, putting the other letters on my desk and turning the thick, textured square over in my hands. My name was written in full cursive on the front: *Jennifer Anne Pierce*, it said; *and Guest*.

I looked up at Carly. "You getting married?"

"No such luck," she said and tapped the envelope with a square forefinger. "You're going to like this one. The Twins are throwing a party."

"The *Twins* are throwing a party?" I repeated in stark disbelief. "Has anyone told them it's winter ?"

Carly shrugged—a gesture that draws the eye to her most prominent features. "Read and weep," she advised, and sashayed away, Earth Mother hips swinging.

I slid my finger under the flap and opened the envelope. The *Wimsy Voice* is owned by John and Jerry Talbot— Jay-Two, Tee-Two, as they are known to certain of their fond employees—who reside in sunny Phoenix, Arizona, and make three or four lightning trips to Maine every year, always during the summer. They acquired the newspaper from Barbara and Tilden Rancourt, who had never been further south than Portland until they retired, sold the paper and moved to Miami on the proceeds.

Since we were now officially embarked upon winter, the *Voice* should have been safe from the Twins until at least May.

You are invited, read the pretty silver script, *to a Christmas party to be held at the Mill Hotel on Friday, December 15, from eight until midnight. Black tie. Open bar.*

"*Black tie?*" I demanded incredulously and heard Carly give her trademark "Hah!" of laughter behind me.

"Don't you have a black tie, Ms. Pierce?" That was Bill Jacques. I spun my chair to face him, across the aisle and down.

"There's peyote in the tap water in Phoenix."

"Could be," Bill allowed judiciously.

"How can they think anybody's going to come to this thing?" I demanded, waving the card for emphasis. "Black tie? Most of the guys in the press room are doing well to have a tie. Period."

"They'll come all right," he said, looking at me over

his half-glasses. "You get to the part about 'open bar'?"

I sighed, hard, and glared at him. "*Why?*"

"Now, that," said my editor, "is a home question. We'll make a reporter out of you yet."

"I'm going to win the lottery," I told him loftily. "And live a life of ease and comfort. In the Caribbean." I spun around to face my desk.

"I think it's nice," Sue Danforth said softly from my right. She had pushed close to the half-wall that separated our desks, and was looking at me seriously. "I mean, the Twins have owned this paper for almost five years and they've never made any effort to–to get to know the staff, or to–to find out what people think, how to improve things . . ." She smiled at me, nervously. "Maybe they've turned over a new leaf, you know? Decided to–take an interest."

"I guess it's possible," I said, since, theoretically, anything is.

She nodded vigorously. "I think that's it. They've decided to get more involved with us here–make a difference. And they've decided throwing a Christmas party is a good way to–to . . ." she floundered.

"To soften us up," I finished. She looked doubtful, but nodded again.

"That's right." She pushed her chair back. "I think it's a good sign," she said firmly, and stood up.

"Well, I hope you're right," I said, while privately considering a black tie affair at the swankiest establishment in town the least efficient way of softening up the *Voice*'s staff. A pizza-and-beer party at the local sports bar, now . . .

I smiled up at Sue. "Have a good night. Say hi to Molly for me."

"I will. Thanks for taking care of that story."

"No problem."

" 'Night," she said and was gone.

Shaking my head, I began to open the rest of my mail.

*

As predicted, the Comprehensive Plan Committee's recommendations were dull as ditchwater. I dutifully took notes in between knocking back two Styrofoam cups of truck-stop coffee lightened with non-dairy powder, then went out into the frigid windy blackness of eight p.m. and got into my car.

The car is new—a replacement for the one I totaled, back in mid-October. A black Camaro, genus Z28, with the five-point-seven liter V8 engine. Electronic automatic transmission. Rear-wheel drive. Platinum-tipped spark plugs. Anti-lock brakes. Stereo CD player. Plush red bucket seats.

You'd have to work a bit to produce a stupider car for slogging through a Maine winter, and I loved it like my own child.

I pulled the seatbelt tight, turned the key, brought up the lights and rolled silently out of the dark lot. I drifted through downtown at precisely the 25-mile-an-hour limit and pulled behind the police station, slipping between two Town of Wimsy cruisers.

Ken Aube lifted a hand as I came in.

"Nice night," he offered, over the squawk of the dispatch box.

"If you like freezing wind," I agreed. "Anything new on the log?"

"Nothing much. This time of year, the town just sort of settles down to freeze." He moved his massive shoulders. "It'll get busy nearer to Christmas, New Year's. Then we'll all go to sleep again 'til spring."

Small town life. Wimsy's cop log hardly ever ran longer than a dozen events, and a murder or rape was front page news that got everyone exclaiming and excited. Far different from the paper in my home town, which had simply stopped reporting rapes: Too common; too tedious.

I went over to the dispatch station, weaving around

the computer boxes that had been stacked in various not-really-out-of-the-way spots for the past three months.

I nodded to the earphoned dispatcher, who pushed the log book toward me without raising her eyes from the paperback romance she was reading.

"You got anybody to install these things yet?" I asked Ken over my shoulder, flipping log pages until I came to the pencil tick showing where Milt had stopped that afternoon.

"Matter of fact, we do," said Ken, as I wrote down that Barry Grenier had been summoned on a charge of assault. I looked over my shoulder.

"Who? If you don't mind my asking."

It would be some so-called pro out of Portland, I thought. It always was. A pro out of Portland had gotten them into this mess in the first place, ordering up a bunch of expensive network computers for the cop station—and disappearing when it came down to the nitty-gritty of actually installing the idiot things. It was my own private opinion that the computers would be found to be seconds or random fire-sale discards when opened, and not an integrated network at all. Which would be just too bad: The Town had spent a lot of money on this system, not to mention the consultant's fee.

"New guy in town," Ken was saying, taking a swig out of his Big Apple Convenience Store plastic mug. "Heard he was from Texas." He put the mug down with a sigh. "Foxwell, I think his name is."

Well, why not? I thought. The Town of Wimsy might as well pay Fox as a fraudulent pro from Portland.

"I hope he can make some sense out of it for you," I said to Ken.

He shrugged. "Don't know what we need the damn' thing for anyhow," he said. "Got along without it this long."

"Welcome to the twentieth century," I said with a grin. "The Information Highway has just put a ramp into Wimsy."

"Just what we need," Ken grunted. "More speeders."

I laughed and went back to the log, noting a High Street

resident had reported a boy throwing stones at her parked car and that a woman on Spring Street had been playing her stereo too loud.

"Well," I said eventually, dutifully checking off the last entry I had noted and flipping my notebook closed. "That's that." I threaded my way through the boxes to Ken's desk and dawdled there a second until he looked up.

"Know anything about the hit-and-run up by the high school?"

He shrugged. "Not my shift."

And no scuttlebutt, I added silently. Or none that Ken was willing to share.

"OK," I said equitably. "See you later."

"Stay warm."

3

The State Police didn't have anything new on the hit-and-run and, according to the spokesman at headquarters, weren't likely to get anything new.

"That time of day, that stretch of road . . ." He paused and I could picture him shaking his head. "Unless there was somebody walking right behind her, or somebody driving the opposite direction happened to look in their mirror . . . We're still asking around. But it looks like we're going to have to get lucky." He sighed, lightly. "Sometimes we get lucky."

The hospital was even less encouraging. Angel Bolduc was still unconscious, her condition guarded. I hung the phone up and went over to lean on the half-wall behind Bill Jacques' computer. He glanced up over the rims of his glasses, fingers still pattering along his keyboard.

"The kid who was hit is in guarded condition— unconscious," I said, and my voice sounded tired in my own ears. Tired and grim. "Hospital's only giving the bare bones. You want me to call her parents?"

Bill's fingers stopped moving. He pulled his glasses off, leaned back in his chair and crossed his arms over his chest, frowning up into my face.

"What've you got?"

I shrugged. "Preliminary report Sue got this afternoon. State cops don't have anything–don't think they will have anything, unless somebody unexpected comes forward with an eyewitness report. Hospital's telling me what I just told you."

He nodded, which only meant he'd heard me, and stared off beyond my shoulder for a couple seconds.

"Send it over," he said, abruptly uncrossing his arms

and resettling his glasses. "It's Sue's story. She can follow up tomorrow."

"Right."

I slid into the chair at second desk, opened "Run", added my couple lines of non-information and ran the spell-check. Then I closed the file, copied it, reformatted the copy, saved it and hit control-alt-S, the sequence that in a just world would transmit the story from Sue's computer to Bill and Carly's network.

"Coming across now," I announced to the room at large. "Run-point-Sue."

"Got it!" Carly called, then: "Down to thirty."

Another miracle of the electronic age accomplished. I shut down Sue's computer and turned out the desk lamp, then moved to my desk and did the same before going back to the cloakroom.

The parka's zipper went up easy, for a change. I stopped by Bill Jacques' computer on my way out.

"Questions on any of that?" I asked, fingering the car keys out of my pocketbook.

He shook his head without raising his eyes. "Looks clean."

"See you tomorrow."

"Good-night."

I waved to Carly, walked past Sports and Features—both dark at eleven-thirty on a wintery Tuesday night—down the hall, down the stairs and for the last time tonight, out into the cold.

*

I parked the Camaro in the barn, walked up the dark, unheated ell, pushed open the plank door and stepped into the kitchen.

Jasper the cat blinked at me from the middle of the kitchen table.

"C'mon, cat, you know the rules," I said, peeling out of the parka and hanging it on its peg. "Get down."

He did, leisurely, and sauntered over to his plate, which was empty, of course.

"Going to put you out in the barn," I told him, bending down for plate and water dish. "Going to make you catch mice for your dinner."

Jasper did not dignify this with a response. He did follow me to the counter and amuse himself by stropping against my legs while I ran water into the bowl and measured cat crunchies onto the plate, purring loudly all the while.

Jasper had been my Aunt Jen's cat and she had left him to me, along with the farmhouse, the ten acres, and the gravel pit. Harry Pelletier, who had lately taken it upon herself to instruct me in the various uses to which the resources of my land might be put, is very taken with the gravel pit. She seems to be even fonder of it than she is of the ancient grove of cedar down by the river.

"Get some money for that gravel, come winter," she'd said, along back November. "Sell a couple yards to the Town, for the roads."

Which I suppose is a reasonable enough idea, but what do I need with more money? I'm not rich, but I own my house; my job brings in enough for groceries, car payment, books, and music, with a little left over to put against that "rainy day" I devoutly hope will never come.

Besides, I don't want the Town trucks coming in, messing up my land–disturbing things. I like it fine the way it is.

"Sell some of that cedar, now," Harry'd suggested, seeing she was getting nowhere with the gravel pit. "Cedar brings a good price."

But I was a city-dweller, blood and bone, and the acres of trees I had inherited were–well, *holy*.

"Cut down the cedar grove?" I demanded, staring at Harry in disbelief. "For *money*?"

"Money's plenty useful, come to find out," she'd said, looking up at me with a squint in her eye. After a minute, she decided to placate me: "Isn't like you'd have to sell 'em all."

"Isn't like I have to sell *any*," I told her. "I've got a job."

She'd shrugged. "Just take a few out," she urged. "Enough to buy some of them new windows, so you won't have to be running the plastic every winter."

"The plastic works fine," I'd said, icily, but standing in my kitchen—midnight now, with the wind sobbing and the mercury hovering at five—I had to admit that the plastic didn't work as fine as all that. And this was just this beginning. It was going to get colder—a lot colder—before winter let me go.

"So you get another sweater," I told myself, carrying Jasper's food and water back to the proper place while he cavorted 'round my legs.

I straightened. Jasper gave me one more over-exuberant bump before diving into supper.

"Get some thermals," I continued talking to myself as I went across the chilly kitchen to the refrigerator. "Just like a real Mainer."

I pulled out a bottle of white wine, a block of cheese, carried them to the counter, poured, sliced, and put away. A handful of crackers went onto the cheese plate, then I gathered up my snack and headed for the hall.

"I'm going to pick up my mail," I called to Jasper. He didn't bother to answer.

Upstairs, I let myself into my room—the only room in the house that's different now then when Aunt Jen died—settled the glass and plate and flicked on my computer.

It purred to life, ran a rapid systems check and sat waiting patiently while I had a sip of wine and a nibble of cheese.

I'd hit the Net first, I thought, and collect my mail. Then I'd check in at *Random Access*. And then, if I was as smart as everybody seemed to think I was, I'd go to bed.

*

Mail on the Net was light: An email from Paolo in Argentina; another from Suzanne in London; the latest issue of *Cyberspace Review*, the tongue-in-cheek "hyper-mag" that served as gossip rag and newspaper of the virtual community. I downloaded it all for later reading and reply, decided against visiting any of the live-time salons, and logged off.

Two minutes later, my computer was dialing the seven-digit number for *Random Access*. A phone rang, quietly, in the depths of my machine—once, twice. On the third ring, there was a spray of static, a strung-out *beee-eep* as my computer and the host computer negotiated with each other, followed by a chime as the connection was made. My screen went still for a moment, then words began to appear.

Welcome
You have reached
RANDOM ACCESS BBS
A place exactly like
No place you've ever been
Your sysop is
Fox

The screen froze for perhaps half-a-minute, then another line appeared, asking for my full name and password. Dutifully, I provided these and the door to *Random Access* opened wide.

There was mail waiting—a note from Marian Younger asking me to pick up a copy of *Programmable C* for her the next time I was by the Central Processing Unit, Wimsy's home-grown computer store.

Marian will be fourteen years old on New Year's day. She's confined to a wheelchair and is fascinated by computers. For awhile, her attention seemed focused on hardware—repair and installation of the actual *machine* of the computer—but over the last month I've seen a shift of interest toward software—

the brains that tell the machine what to do. I suspect Fox has had something to do with that.

I wrote a quick reply, telling Marian I would buy the book tomorrow and drop it off Friday after she was home from school, unless she needed it sooner. Two keystrokes mailed the note and I moved on to the main board–the Speakeasy.

Today's first message was from Skip Leterneau, a regular, though one who had heretofore been more interested in the substantial file areas than the social chit-chat of the Speakeasy. Skip had lately been reading up on a new notion in hydroelectric dams, which would utilize an air turbine and require significantly less head–fall of water–in order to work. He apparently found the concept terribly exciting and went on at length, waxing nearly poetical in the density of his technical description. I reached the end and heaved a sigh of relief.

The next message was from Lisa Gagnon. I reached for my wine and had a sip.

Lisa had reached *Random Access* days after her eight-month marriage had fallen messily apart, a circumstance she blamed almost entirely on having lost her job as a stitcher at the Welltread Shoe factory. Lisa had worked at the factory for five years, but during the six months prior to her firing had experienced trouble making her daily quota. She claimed her hands bothered her–fingers numb; wrists achy. Her shift boss chose to believe otherwise and Lisa was out of a job.

Shortly thereafter, her truck driver husband packed his clothes and moved out, leaving behind his wife, his ancient Tandy computer and very little else.

All, however, was not lost: The Tandy had a working modem in it. Carl, owner and chief tech at CPU, gave Lisa the number to *Random Access*. And Lisa was hooked.

Over the couple months she had been a regular user of the board, Lisa had regaled the rest of us with painstakingly detailed synopses of her days–days so dismal, so full of rejection and self-doubt, that I for one counted it a miracle that she hadn't simply turned her face to the wall and called it quits.

We heard how she was denied unemployment benefits because her former employer stated she'd been fired for cause. We heard about having to fill out the form for food stamps and how nice that lady had been, at least.

We heard how the Town refused to give her a tank of oil when winter came howling into Wimsy in mid-November. And a few days later, we heard how the oil truck came down to the trailer and the driver told her it was all paid, but wouldn't tell her who had paid it, so she couldn't even thank the person—her "good angel", as she had it.

We heard how there was a waiting list for the job retraining classes and how the Federal money was running out. We heard about the dismal, dismal job market, and the people who were cruel to her when she walked in, cold, to ask for work.

I put the wine glass down, wondering what today's disaster was going to be. Hoping that maybe the "good angel" had come through with another minor miracle to lighten Lisa's load . . .

I GOT A JOB!!!!

The message shouted, almost deafening in reflected joy and relief.

It's at the Mill and I'm going to be cleaning rooms, mostly, but they're going to train me to do other things—coat check and maybe front desk and maybe they'll teach me how to wait tables in the restaurant. I've got a friend says the tips are wicked good. I start tomorrow morning and I GOT A JOB!!

The rest of the messages were notes of congratulation from other users, urging her to get plenty of sleep and leave early so she would make a good impression her first day at work. I added a note of my own, telling her how happy I was for her–which looked trite on the screen, but the truth was that I *was* happy for her–not to mention relieved and somewhat ashamed. That someone could be so *joyful* over landing a job cleaning hotel rooms after living through two months of concentrated hell . . . I shook my head and closed my letter, glancing at the clock at the corner of my screen.

"Bedtime, Jen," I told myself and moved my hand toward <G> for <G>oodbye.

The screen broke–reformed into a plain blue playing field, bisected by a thin white line. Letters appeared–quickly, smoothly–beneath the line.

Good evening, Jennifer.

I smiled and typed. *Fox. Don't you ever sleep?*

Certainly, he typed back. *Don't you?*

As often as I can, I answered, and then: *I see Lisa's finally had some good luck.*

It's about time, Fox commented. *I hope this is just the first of many positive reverses. I've noticed that having a job tends to make many things easier.*

Speaking of jobs, I said, *I hear you've landed a plum, yourself.*

There was a moment of hesitation, then: *The police station. That's quick work, Jennifer. I only got the final approval this evening.*

I saw Ken Aube tonight and he already had the scuttlebutt, I told him, grinning. *There are no secrets in a small town, Mr. Foxwell.*

So I begin to learn. Tell me, what do you know about the former consultant?

I didn't know much–my fingers danced across the keys, giving Fox the little I had.

His name is John Custer and his office is in Portland. He wore a suit and tie and talked the talk. Carl's pissed at him because he ordered all the stuff himself instead of going through CPU. He milked the analysis part of the contract for all it was worth, then booked when the machines hit town.

I hesitated, then added, *I didn't get the idea he knew what he was doing.*

A fine mess I've gotten myself into, Fox typed, and I could almost hear his sigh through the screen.. *Ah, well. Isn't penance good for the soul?*

You're asking me?

Jennifer, you really have too low an opinion of yourself. Am I keeping you?

I hesitated. *I should go,* I typed reluctantly, then thought of something else. *Fox?*

Yes.

Marian asked me to pick her up a copy of Programmable C. Is that a good place for her to start or are there other books I should get for her while I'm at Carl's?

There was a pause and I leaned back in my chair, reaching for my wine. I'd had a sip and replaced the glass before he began to type again.

If you don't mind, I'd like to talk to her before you buy any books. C can be a bit of a bear, and in any case it's not the place to begin. There's a . . . progression of study. Like math.

Sure, I typed. *Talk to her. After all, you're the resident expert.*

A dubious honor, I suspect, Fox returned. *Good night, Jennifer. Sleep well.*

Good night, Fox, I typed, and the bisected screen was gone, replaced by *Random Access'* main menu.

I touched <G> for <G>oodbye and the board logged me off.

NO CARRIER, my computer reported and I sighed lightly, for no reason that I could name, and shut down for the night.

4

My usual schedule is Sunday through Thursday, with Friday and Saturday off.

But not this Friday.

This Friday, I was assigned to cover the JUST SAY NO TO DRUGS, WIMSY! rally at the high school, Milt Vane having turned the job down cold.

Sometimes, I wonder how Milt Vane got to be first desk.

The rally was set for seven o'clock. I arrived at six-thirty, parked the Camaro in the bus loop behind an old Chevy van and walked across the wide pavement, toward the light spilling from the big front doors. It was snowing tonight—spiteful little spits of ice that stung my face and melted the instant they hit cement.

The banner stretched across the lobby was black, with JUST SAY NO TO DRUGS! in bright red letters. There were about two dozen assorted students and adults about, all wearing the intent expressions of people who suspect they've forgotten something vital. I saw Dan Skat, the *Voice's* photographer, over by the far wall and moseyed in that direction.

"Hey, Jen."

"Hey, yourself. I thought this was your day off."

He grinned. "My daughter's dance class is on the program, so I figured, since I had to be here anyway . . ."

"You might as well get paid for it," I finished and nodded. "I understand entirely. Now, if Milt had your work ethic—"

"We'd be living in a whole different world," Dan said, shaking his head. "I wonder how long Bill's going to let him play prima donna before he brings down the boom."

He straightened suddenly, like a cat hearing the sound

of a can opener touching a tuna can, and swung his camera into position. I craned my head around looking for what he'd seen, and spied a tallish blonde in a green parka, tight black jeans and high black boots sweeping into the lobby. The parka was unzipped, showing the shine of gold lame beneath.

"Who's that?" I asked Dan.

"Peggy Neuman," he said, naming Wimsy's own rock legend. "See you later, Jen."

"Right," I said, but Dan was already gone, stalking his celebrity obliquely through the bustle.

I unzipped my own parka, made certain of notebook and Bic, settled my pocketbook more comfortably across my shoulder and surveyed the situation.

It was now quarter to show time and the audience was beginning to arrive. Six high school kids took up stations by the busy doors, handing out flyers that had been photocopied onto the ever-popular goldenrod paper. I went forward, moving against the crowd, and claimed a program from a boy with a buzz cut and a varsity sweater.

"Just say no," he told me, serious as stone.

"No," I said obediently, and slipped the flyer from between his fingers with a smile.

*

Forty-five minutes and several presentations later–including a close personal chat with Varny the Drug-Sniffing Dog and his partner, Trooper Ron of the Maine State Police–I put the Bic in my lap and carefully flexed my fingers. On-stage, the denizens of Darby's Dance Studio were performing a parable for our times.

In turn, each child in the troupe was approached by a single child in a black T-shirt emblazoned, front and back, with a bright yellow DRUGS. All, after an inexpertly but enthusiastically pantomimed struggle with their conscience, resisted the blandishments of the black-clad child, who turned out to be none other than Abby, Dan Skat's nine-year-old.

Finally, all the children who had Said No looked at each other, counted their numbers, and turned as one to look at the solitary dusky figure in the center of the stage. DRUGS shifted nervously. The mob moved one step forward. DRUGS prudently did not pause to negotiate: She turned tail and exited, running, stage left, whereupon all the Say-Noers cheered, joined hands and danced an exuberant ring-around-the-rosy before also darting off, stage left. Applause was long and good-natured.

Deep in my center aisle seat, I sighed and looked about me. The auditorium was packed–adults, children, old people–and everyone seemed to be having a wicked good time. Earlier, I'd seen Harry Pelletier and Morris DuChamp jockeying for seats front and center. Harry'd been wearing a black baseball cap with DARE emblazoned in strident orange italics just above the peak. Morris had a button instructing the world to DARE TO KEEP KIDS OFF DRUGS pinned to the front of his good wool coat.

Well, I thought, *as entertainment we're doing fine.* But did this kind of community feeding frenzy actually keep kids off dope? I had my doubts.

Around me, the applause pattered down, the crowd settled, voices easing, chairs creaking slightly as people hunched forward in their places. I glanced at the flyer on my knee: last act of the evening.

Peggy Neuman, the listing ran, *rhythm and rap.*

I sat up a little straighter, myself.

The house lights dimmed and the audience sound went down, too, like it was wired to the same rheostat. A spot lanced out of the growing murk and made a bull's eye in the center of the stage, waiting.

The silence was broken by a child's shrill question, quickly shushed.

And from the darkness of stage right came a blonde woman in black jeans and a glittering golden shirt. She carried a wooden stool in one hand and a battered, big-bellied acoustic guitar in the other.

Unhurriedly, she crossed the stage to the spot, set the stool upright with an effortless swing of her arm, then smiled over the dark auditorium before she sat down, hitched one leg up and got the guitar into position.

"Hi, there," she said, and her voice was a mellow alto, husky along the edges, as if she smoked, or used to. She ran her fingers over the strings, testing their mettle, shook her head at a sour note.

"I'm Peggy Neuman," she said, working the pin and the string. Once again, she looked out over the audience she couldn't see. "Some of you know me. I grew up on the Town Farm Road–didn't quite graduate from the old high school, downtown." There was a flutter of laughter at that; up on the stage, she grinned.

"That's all right," she said, trying the strings again. This time, the chording pleased her and she nodded, blonde hair curving along the line of her cheek.

"So, anyway," she said, crossing her arms on the guitar and leaning toward us. "I been out of town awhile–twenty, twenty-two years. Since I've been back home, people've been stopping me on the street–" she paused and aimed a slow grin outward. "I forgot how that happens, in a town like Wimsy." There was an appreciative ruffle of laughter from the audience.

"People stop me on the street," Peggy Neuman continued, "and they ask me where I've been and what I've done and I've tried to say, but it's hard to fit everything in, standing between the IGA and the parking lot, with the wind off the Smoke freezing your ears and other delicate parts." More laughter. I smiled in the deeps of my seat and the woman on stage nodded easily, companionably.

"What I thought I'd do tonight, while I have you all in one place–" She paused, letting the laugh run through while she fingered the strings and ghosted out the beginning of a line. "I thought I'd tell you where I've been and what I've been doing—and I hope you'll take it to heart."

The ghost line solidified, spinning out into the quiet, a silvery cable of rhythm. She let it build until it could almost be seen against the dark, and then she began.

I would have called it talking blues rather than rap, but why quibble? The lady was a master, and she had the whole place in her hand.

"The things I done, the things I seen," was the irregular refrain. We heard how she left home at seventeen, joined her first band, got introduced to grass—"just a little toke, now and then, to feel the music cleaner." How she formed her own band and made a name, did gigs and cut records, how the booze got important, and the dope even more, how she ran out on her marriage, and how her band finally left her.

"But I didn't quit, then, oh my no. I could still look *down* and see bottom."

This being a teaching parable, she *did* hit bottom. We heard about the horrors of kicking cocaine. We heard about the daily grind of AA. We heard how, straight, she pulled together another band and began again, until one of her band members died of an overdose—how she took that as a sign, and came home.

"The things I seen, the things I done," she sighed within her spotlight, and flattened her palm on the strings before looking out over the dark, silent audience. "And I'm one of the lucky ones."

The audience was absolutely silent. On stage, Peggy Neuman stood, a long-legged, deep-bosomed blonde in black and gold, holding a beat-up guitar by the neck. She bowed into the silence, and straightened.

"It's good to be home," she said, and without further fanfare walked off into the blackness of stage left.

More silence, for a long beat of three. I dropped the Bic into my lap, raised my hands and began to clap.

Two seconds later, the rest of the audience joined in.

5

It was nine-thirty when I left the *Voice*, hauling hard against the outside door until I heard the night latch snap home, then paused in the meager protection of the entryway, car keys in hand and irritated by the vague notion that I was forgetting something.

Upstairs, I'd had the newsroom to myself. I wrote my story on Bill Jacques' computer, and left a petunia-pink sticky note in the middle of his monitor, the file name carefully printed in purple letters. I stayed a couple minutes longer, cleaning up odds and ends, then pulled on the parka and headed out.

So, then. Nine-thirty of a blustery Friday evening. Time for Jen Pierce, girl reporter, to return to the house on Wimsy Point and feed her–

"Oh, hell," I said to the cold darkness. "Cat food."

The Wimsy IGA had been closed for half-an-hour, as had the rest of town, except those places that shut down earlier.

"Waterville, here I come," I said with a sigh, and headed across the parking lot toward the Camaro.

*

There were a dozen or so cars and trucks clustered close to the doors of the 24-hour Shop 'n Save in Waterville's Elm Plaza. I pulled in between a red Ford Tempo and an old Dart showing body rot like leprosy under the vapor pink lights.

Inside, I unzipped the parka, shifted my pocketbook to my right shoulder and began a leisurely tour of the premises. Cat food was aisle four, clear across the store, but I figured it would still be there in fifteen minutes or so, after I'd worked the kinks out of my legs.

I toured Produce and Seafood, skirted the live lobster

tank and turned up Condiments.

Fox was half-way up the aisle, reaching for a bottle of salad dressing.

Life is full of ironies. It wasn't all that long ago that I desperately needed to locate Fox and had no hope of finding him. Now, it seems I meet him everywhere.

Bottle in hand, he turned from the shelf toward his basket, saw me, and smiled his slight smile.

"Hello, Jennifer."

"Hi," I said, my own smile feeling ridiculously wide.

Fox bent over his basket and deposited the salad dressing, his movements unhurried and graceful. Straightening, he put his long hands along the push bar and cocked his head.

"Shopping or touring?" he asked.

"Both," I admitted, stepping aside to let him move the basket forward. "Mission objective is cat food, but I wanted to walk out the rally before I went home."

"Rally?" We were shoulder-to-shoulder now, and it seemed perfectly natural to turn and walk with him, back the way I'd come.

"The Say No To Drugs Rally at the high school," I explained and sighed. "It was about what you'd expect–skits from the kids and a friendly chat from the state trooper attached to the drug dog. But the last act . . ." I shook my head while Fox paused to take aboard a jar of spicy brown mustard.

"The last act was a bomb?" he asked, slanting a cobalt-blue glance at me from beneath thick auburn lashes.

I looked at him and took a breath. "The last act," I said, "was incredible. A woman named Peggy Neuman–" I let it drift off, at a loss to describe the song–the power.

"I've seen her a couple times at the Chez," Fox said, naming Waterville's best–and roughest–live music club. "The lady is very good."

"Very good," I agreed. "And very brave. I don't think I'd have the guts to stand up in front of the town I grew up in and lay out all my mistakes."

"Maybe she thinks she can keep someone else from making the same mistakes," Fox murmured as we reached the end of the aisle.

"She said that. I just hope they don't–" *crucify her*, I was going to say, because with a small town you can never tell who'll be a hero and who'll be the goat.

But I never got a chance to finish the sentence.

Fox pushed his basket to the left, apparently meaning to go up Baking Needs. A flicker of sable in the corner of my eye was all the warning either of us got before Janice Younger erupted on the scene.

With her fur jacket snugged tight at her tiny waist, her black hair cunningly wind-tousled, and her pink-and-cream complexion, she looked gorgeous, as always. Also as always, she spared me one disdainful glance from eyes as green and as hard as emeralds before closing in on her intended prey.

"David!" she cried, in accents of ringing joy. She pressed a perfectly manicured hand to her fur-encased bosom. "How *wonderful* to see you again!"

It's a source of amazement to me, that Janice Younger remains as yet unmurdered by an outraged Significant Other.

Janice is accustomed to adoration. She is accustomed to a certain, shall we say, slavish gratitude from the men she chooses to honor with her notice. I have seen grown men— mature, stable men–drawn across a busy room by a flutter of soot-black lashes, to be held by the goddess' side, sometimes for hours, while the abandoned wife or lady friend of the ensorcelled seethed and steamed and tried, usually unsuccessfully, to pretend there was nothing amiss.

Adoration and impotent fury–these are the emotions Janice Younger most commonly awakens. She neither inspires, nor is accustomed to meeting, indifference.

Which is why I will treasure the look of startled blankness that passed over Fox's face for a long, long time.

In a heartbeat, he had placed her. I like to think it was the resemblance to Marian that clued him in.

"Mrs. Younger," he said, with Fox-like gravity. She extended a hand and lay it tremulously along his sleeve, face uptilted, green eyes dewy and soft.

"Janice. Please."

"Janice," Fox repeated, and something in his tone persuaded me that he had utterly forgotten her given name. He stepped back from the basket, neatly slipping away from her hand, and glanced over to me, cobalt eyes a trifle wide. "Jennifer, this is—"

"Oh, Jenny and I are *well* acquainted," Janice assured him. "She and Marian are such good friends! So much in common!" She smiled dazzlingly up into his face.

"I see," Fox said, and even Janice caught the dry note on the edge of his voice. She smiled again, a little wistfully, dropped her eyes and stepped aside.

"I don't want to keep you," she said, demure now and almost as grave as he. "I know you're a very busy man. I just wanted to make sure that you knew you were always welcome at the house. Stop by *any*time."

Fox inclined his head. "Thank you," he said seriously. "You're very kind."

She copied his gesture, bowing her head as chastely as a nun, and went one more step aside before throwing me another hard green glance.

"Good-night, Jenny," she said, too sweetly.

"Good-night," I said evenly, and followed Fox up Baking Needs.

He paused in the flour section and bent to pick up a sack of cornmeal, then stood holding it in his hand while he fished the gold-rimmed glasses out of his breast pocket, opened them with a practiced flick of the wrist and slid them onto his nose.

"You don't go by—Jenny—do you?" he asked, voice excruciatingly even as he frowned down at the recipes printed on the brown paper sack.

"Jennifer, or Jen, if I get a choice." I shrugged. "I

don't usually get a choice. Most people just assume 'Jenny.' It's not really worth fighting about."

He nodded, pulled the glasses off, folded and stowed them in one fluid motion, then bent and put the cornmeal back. He turned to face me across the cart.

"I met her for five minutes this afternoon," he said, and it was bewilderment in the eyes. With Fox, you have to watch the eyes. "When I went to see Marian."

"Guess you made an impression," I said, trying for lightness. He shook his head, eyes level on mine and not moving.

"The first time I visited Marian," he said, as if it explained something, "back in October. I met her father. It seemed to me that he was living there."

I shrugged. "If it doesn't bother them, I don't guess it should bother you."

I don't always think before I talk, a trait that's gotten me in so much trouble in my life you'd expect I'd've learned better by now. Fox's eyes widened, shock showing along the edges of bewilderment, and I glanced aside, feeling like a certified heel.

"I'm sorry," I muttered, then sighed sharply and forced myself to look back at him.

"See," I said, taking refuge in the patient, non-judgmental secretary-voice I'd learned years ago; "it's nothing personal. It's just . . . Some people collect dolls, OK? Janice collects men." I shook my head, unsure of what else I should say–what he wanted me to say. "Everybody knows it."

"Everyone except the new collectible on the block," Fox commented with unexpected bitterness. He put a hand up to comb the hair off his forehead. "Thank you."

I hesitated, wondering if this were sarcasm; if I had–another of my specialties–failed some arcane test of friendship and was now dismissed . . .

"No," Fox said gravely. "I mean it, Jennifer. Thank you." He went to the back of the basket, put his hands on the bar, and paused.

"I'm new around here," he said, and offered me one of his slender smiles. "I'd appreciate any help you can give me."

I smiled, absurdly relieved, and turned to walk beside him again. "I'm nothing but a flatlander, myself," I told him, and grinned. "There's a story about a guy who moved to Maine with his wife when they were in their twenties. Ten or twelve years later he meets an old Mainer who wants to know if he's a native. And the guy says, 'No, my wife and I are from Away. But my children were born here. They're natives.' To which the old Mainer replies, 'Ayuh. And if yer cat had kittens in the oven, would you call 'em muffins?' "

Fox stopped the basket, eyes wide and dancing. He didn't laugh—I hadn't really *expected* him to laugh, I told myself—but the smile seemed a shade wider than usual.

"I like him—the old Mainer."

"So do I. Unfortunately, there's less and less of them. Maine kids think it's cool to dress like ghetto kids and listen to rap music." I shook my head. "What's rap got to do with Maine? But they see it on MTV and it's not what's around here, so it must be the way to go."

"Welcome to the homogenized society," Fox said, reaching up for a bottle of maple syrup. "We worked hard for this."

"Yeah?" I considered him. "You remember why?"

*

We continued the tour at a leisurely stroll. Fox talked about the police station job and the rare mess he'd found in place.

"I wonder about this consultant," he said, shaking his head. "He specified a Windows LAN—" He threw me a glance, one eyebrow up. "Local—"

"—area network," I finished. "I know."

"Right. He specifies Windows, which a child on the street can tell you needs at least four megabytes of RAM to run properly–and I have at least half of them with two megs–one RAMless wonder–someone cooked the hard drive in that one, too . . ." Another headshake. "And one copy of Windows for Work Groups."

I blinked. "One?"

"I did a recount," he assured me gravely. "One it is. And then I had to explain to the chief of police why I couldn't just install it on all the machines."

I laughed. Fox walks tall–Air Force brat–and in fact matches my own six foot, but Chief Twitchell is *big*, loud and belligerent where Fox is quiet and incisive. I'd have paid twenty bucks for a front row seat during that donnybrook.

"Who won?"

Fox stopped the basket and took on a couple cans of coffee. "I asked Carl to order in half-a-dozen more."

"Wow."

"What I can't understand is this consultant–John Custer. I'm told he came with the very highest credentials–yet he orders in trashed machines, inappropriate machines, one copy of the software. What on earth was the man thinking?"

"He was thinking 'easy money,' " I told him. "People from Portland are always coming up-country to make a killing from the locals."

He looked at me. "Another one of those things everybody knows?"

"No, this is one of the things only flatlanders know and Mainers think you're rude to mention," I said. "Portland's a city, see? So it stands to reason that all good things proceed from it. Of course, if you want the *best* you need to go to Boston."

"I'll remember that."

"See that you do."

We finished out the paper goods aisle in silence, then turned into Pet Food.

"How are things at the paper?" Fox murmured.

"Same as always. There was a hit-and-run out by the

high school that the State cops don't think they're going to get lucky on. Sixteen years old. In a coma at Waterville Hospital." I shook my head, and pushed the grimness aside with a pure effort of will.

"That's the hottest scoop—except for the fact that the owners are giving a black tie affair at the Mill. Command performance for all employees." I sighed. "The press room guys are going to all have to rent tuxes—might rent one, myself." I made a detour across the aisle.

"I have a tux," Fox said as I reached up to pull down Jasper's favorite brand of cat food.

I threw him a grin over my shoulder. "Won't fit, but thanks."

He raised an eyebrow. "I assure you, it fits quite well."

I turned carefully, half-a-dozen cat food boxes trembling in my arms. "What's a computer geek doing with a tux?"

Fox widened his eyes in what I strongly suspected was utterly bogus innocence. "I had to attend an awards banquet."

"And so naturally you bought a tuxedo," I said in a tone of broad enlightenment just as the top three boxes jumped ship. Fox leaned forward, caught them, and dropped them into his basket.

"I have room for the rest, too," he murmured.

"Thanks," I said, and dumped them in, helter-skelter. "It's cheaper to rent a tux than buy one."

He shrugged. "Kathy liked it," he said, which is the third time I've heard him say his dead wife's name since October. "My own mother was pleased to proclaim me 'entirely presentable'—a rare compliment. It was a giddy moment."

I grinned. "Sure it was. And you schlepped this tux all the way to Maine?"

"One never knows," Fox said virtuously, "when the duties of society will overtake one."

"Very true," I was able to concede gravely in a moment or two. "However, this affair might be more profitably considered as a masquerade. The *Wimsy Voice*, its employees, hangers-on and et ceteras are not haute ton."

"Yet an opportunity to wear a tuxedo should not lightly be set aside."

I took a second to consider him: Pointy face serious as always, eyes . . . Intent. Something important was going on—or Fox thought so. And I very much wished that I knew what it was.

"Odds are the party's going to be horrible," I told him, which was the truth as I believed it. "The Twins don't tend to think very highly of anybody who'll work for them."

"I'd never join a club that would have me as a member," Fox murmured. I nodded, with a faint grin to Groucho.

"God only knows why they've taken it into their heads to throw a staff party—but it's the wrong party and it's a couple years too late. You'd be bored to death."

He tipped his head, watching my face. "Will you be bored to death?"

"Well, naturally." I sighed. "But it's my job—I *have* to go. It doesn't mean I have to let you offer yourself up as a human sacrifice."

His lips twitched. "But I might be amused. After all, I don't work for the paper."

"And so might actually be considered human by the real people. It's a possibility," I conceded, and chewed my lip.

"You really want to go to this thing?" I asked finally.

He met my eyes square. "Yes."

"Be it on your head, then," I said dubiously. "I don't want to hear you say I didn't warn you."

"You won't," Fox promised, and smiled.

6

"This is Rand Funeral Home," Thomas Rand's bland voice informed me Sunday evening. "I have an obit."

"Just a second." I opened a new file on the computer, settled the receiver more comfortably between ear and shoulder and wriggled my fingers over the keyboard. "Go ahead."

"Angel Bolduc," he said. "Sixteen. Died Saturday evening at Waterville Hospital of injuries sustained in a traffic accident."

I took it down and all the rest, my fingers mindlessly typing what my ears heard: how Angel had been an honor student, a star player on the varsity ice hockey team, an active member of the Wimsy DARE chapter, and part-time front desk clerk at the Mill. Survivors included her parents, two sisters, maternal grandfather and paternal great-grandmother. A brother, Jonathan Charles, had died last summer.

"Of an overdose of drugs," the bland voice said, momentarily becoming a shade less bland. "The family asked that be included."

I cleared my throat. "Sure," I said, and typed it in.

"In lieu of flowers," Mr. Rand continued, "donations may be sent in her name to the Wimsy chapter of DARE."

I typed that, too, then the visiting hours, the day and time of the funeral.

My fingers came to a rest and I cleared my throat again. "I'd like to read this back to you," I said, "to make sure I haven't missed anything."

"Thank you," Mr. Rand said with unaccustomed courtesy. "I would appreciate that."

I ran the file to the top and began, squinting a little at the wavery, soft-edged letters. At the end of the obit, I closed my eyes entirely.

"Very good," said Mr. Rand. "I may have another later on this evening. How late can I call?"

"Tomorrow's page closes at eight," I heard myself say, calm and professional. "If I know there's an obit coming, I can ask the editor to hold it 'til nine."

There was a thoughtful pause. "That won't be necessary," he decided. "If I don't get back to you before deadline, I'll call it in for Wednesday's paper. Good-night."

"Good-night," I said numbly. Eyes still closed, I cradled the phone, then just sat there, feeling empty and peculiarly light-headed.

Honestly, Jennifer, I told myself, *get a grip. Kids die all the time.* In fact, kids die so often and of such varied causes that I'm sometimes astonished so many do live to grow up.

But this was–different. A kid walking home from school along a stretch of road she'd probably walked every single day; a good kid, a bright kid, obeying the traffic laws, maybe thinking about her homework, or her boyfriend, or the DARE extravaganza she was helping to organize for the high school, when out of nowhere . . .

"Problem, Miz Pierce?"

I started, eyes snapping open and focusing on Bill Jacques' blunt face. He crossed his arms on the rickety divider that separated Sue's desk from mine. "You're looking a trifle peaked, if you don't mind my saying so," he commented.

I swallowed, moved my eyes back to the screen where the obit lurked, in fuzzy yellow letters, the name shimmering at the top of the screen: Angel Bolduc. I looked back at Bill.

"The kid died," I said and my voice cracked. I cleared my throat. "Angel Bolduc. Last night. Never came out of the coma."

He sighed and rubbed at the indentation his glasses had left across the bridge of his nose.

"Rough one," he said, refolding his arms. "That's the same family lost the boy back last June?"

I nodded.

"They must be out of their minds." He sighed again. "Well, nobody said the game was fair." He looked closely into my face. "You going to be OK?"

"I'll be OK," I said, though I was still feeling a tad light-headed.

He nodded and straightened, patting the top of my monitor with a light palm. "Send that over to me when you're done. I'll fill in some stuff and give her a right send-off." He turned. Turned back.

"When's the funeral?"

"Wednesday afternoon."

"That'll be Sue's, then," he said and headed back to his desk.

*

I finished my shift in a kind of gray blear and drove home in the same condition. In the kitchen, I hung pocketbook and parka on pegs, turned, and just stood there, feeling– and probably looking–like a gangly robot that's lost its programming.

"Shit." I raised both hands and combed my hair back hard from my face. When my fingers snagged on wind-knots, I ruthlessly pushed them through, welcoming the minor twinges of pain.

"Get a *grip*," I told myself, speaking loudly in the cold, quiet kitchen. "It's a damn' shame she died, but for God's sake, Jennifer, you didn't even *know* the kid."

What kind of a person do you have to be, Sue Danforth wondered from the edge of my memory, *to hit somebody like that and just drive away?*

It didn't necessarily follow that the person who had hit Angel was evil, or even a garden variety badass. He could have been frightened, or only criminally negligent. And the point was, it *didn't matter* which of those sorts of people or any other had done the deed: Angel had taken her death the instant she'd been struck. It had taken her five days to finish the business, under the best care Waterville Hospital could muster, but if the guy in the truck hadn't happened to glance down into the ditch and spot the red parka, she'd have been dead a little sooner. That was all.

When I was living in Baltimore and working at the university for the second time, I'd formed a friendship of convenience with Professor of Research and Statistics Michael DiSandro, "Stats" as he was known to his intimates.

It is not easy being the only son of an Old School Italian family, and Stats' position was made less comfortable by the fact that there was a considerable inheritance to be lost, did he fail to toe the heterosexual line. So, I "dated" Stats as required for effect, and he returned the favor on the rare occasions when I needed an escort. It was a system that worked so well that we became actual friends, though I did have to place a moratorium on statistics.

Michael DiSandro's pure passion in life was statistics. He would quote, jiggle and juggle them for hours. He'd talk variances and covariances through cocktails, dinner and the play, if left unchecked, and never could understand why no one else seemed to find his numbers as delightful and clever as he did himself.

One of the statistical lines he kept close tabs on was the mortality rate of Baltimore City children, ages six to eighteen. The project had started as an "exercise," he told me, but soon took on an urgency of its own.

"They're dying in droves out there, Jen—drive-bys, overdoses, traffic accidents, beatings, burnings, drownings, starvation, and sheer stupidity." He'd shaken his head and knocked back a slug of Walker Red. "I wouldn't be sixteen again for anything you could name. It's worse than a jungle out there. It's a war zone."

But that had been Baltimore—a big, tough, urban sprawl that sucked in lives like a black hole sucks in light. This was Maine—Wimsy, Maine, population 3,212. People were safe in

Wimsy.

Wrong.

People in Maine want to believe they're safe, that murder and rape and drug dealing are problems belonging to the make-believe land of Away. There are so few murders in Maine, thirty-seven in 1988, that each one can be–and is–held up for public scrutiny and censured as the act of a monster. Rape is a little more popular–243 reported in a state-wide population of one-million-two. Drugs–drugs are worming their way in, though no one seems to know how quickly or exactly how much. Just like drugs everywhere.

The fact is that no place is "safe". People die everywhere. Not even an honor student from Wimsy High School is immune.

A gust of wind hit the side of the house, shaking the windows like so many loose teeth. I jumped, shivering in a sudden runnel of icy air, and my eye snagged on the clock above the refrigerator.

Twelve forty-five.

"Time for bed, Jen," I told myself, trying to ignore the fact that I did not feel in the least bit sleepy.

Deliberately, I marched across the kitchen, snapped off the light and climbed the stairs.

"C'mon, Jasper," I called out, as if I wasn't certain he was already nested in the quilts and snoozing. "Bedtime!"

*

The right to bear arms MUST NOT be given away! I read an hour later, sleep having after all been impossible.

Mark Bernier was almost as fond of exclamation points as he was of his extensive collection of firearms. He was normally one of the quieter citizens of *Random Access*, but every once in a while somebody somewhere made a noise that sounded like "gun control" and Mark dragged out his cybersoapbox and jumped aboard. The proximate cause this time seemed to be the President's proposal to institute a waiting period for the purchase of bullets.

The Minutemen had no bullets!! Mark told us. *But they had silver and pewter and the need to defend their country!!! A waiting period for bullets will no more keep a REAL AMERICAN from readiness than that same lack kept the Minutemen out of war!*

Mark's tirade ended with **KEEP THE FAITH!!!** and I breathed a sigh of relief before I scrolled down to the next message. It was from Lisa, in response to Mark's pro-gun advertisement.

I HATE guns, she stated, with un-Lisalike abruptness. *I don't think anybody needs to carry a gun. Not even policemen or soldiers. If there weren't any guns, then we wouldn't need to have policemen or soldiers and if everybody ate cows and chickens and fish then nobody would need guns to hunt. Hunting's cruel. Guns are cruel. My husband had a gun and I made him get rid of it when we got married. I won't live in a house with a gun. I think the government should take all the guns away from everybody and melt them all down to make cars out of. Lisa.*

And so there, I thought, blinking at the screen in slight bemusement. This was not the first anti-gun message I'd seen from Lisa—her rhapsodies against the cruelty of guns and hunting had hit a crescendo during deer hunting season, back in November—but it was by far the most coherent. I'd gotten the impression through reading her various notes on the subject that Lisa was more than merely gunshy; she was a gun-phobe. She'd stated on more than one occasion that the mere sight of a gun made her sick to her stomach.

I sighed and touched the key to scroll on to the next message. Fanatics of any flavor make me uneasy. I was no more comfortable with Lisa's sentiments—though I did find a certain charm in the suggestion that cars be fabricated from melted guns—than I was with Mark's ready-on-the-right rhetoric. *Middle of the road Jen,* I thought, *always wants the world in balance*

. . .

The next message was from Skip Leterneau, addressed to "All Users."

Hi, there. I'm with the mitten project and would like to ask anybody who has any yarn to donate to leave me a message here. I can pick it up or you can leave it at the library or at the co-op or at Skip's Skis if you're in the neighborhood. It doesn't have to be a lot of yarn, a skein makes a difference, but I can't use any little ends. The children thank you for your help. **SKIP**

Oops. I'd forgotten all about that. I pulled a pad of paper out of my desk drawer and made a note to buy a couple skeins of wool and leave them at Mother's Pantry co-op for Skip to pick up.

Skip's was the last message. The clock in the upper right-hand corner of my screen read 01:56:59 a.m., time and enough to seek my bed and court sleep once more, if Angel Bolduc would let me. I moved my finger toward <G> for Goodbye.

The screen shimmered, broke and reformed into the familiar chat field.

Jennifer, it's two o'clock in the morning.

I grinned and shook my head while my fingers danced across the keys in response. *But I know where my cat is. Where do you get off yelling about my bedtime, anyway? *You* pulled *me* into chat.*

Touché, Fox acknowledged. *I don't suppose you'll believe I'm typing in my sleep?*

Not at that speed. What's up?

I'm working on a project. Thought I had a breakthrough—about five hours ago. I just looked up and saw you on the board and thought I'd say hello and ask you what on earth a mitten project is.

I grinned. *It's a Good Work. Some of the memes—the grandmothers—and other good-workers knit mittens. Dozens and dozens of pairs of mittens. Check out the library and the*

IGA—they usually put up their mitten trees along about Thanksgiving. By a couple weeks before Christmas there are mitten boxes all over town. The idea is that if a kid loses his pair all he has to do is find a mitten box and take another pair. Skip's got a late start this year—must've been busy up at the shop.

Skip knits mittens? Fox inquired, dubiously—or so it seemed to me.

That's right. I hear his sister Julia used to be the champion Wimsy knitter, but she married four or five years ago and moved to Skowhegan. Skip does pretty well—couple dozen mittens a year, usually. Not too bad for a guy who runs a small engine repair shop.

Not bad at all, Fox agreed. *Thank you, Jennifer.*

No problem. I answered, and changed the subject. *What do you think about Lisa's idea of melting all the guns down for automobiles?*

I think it an interesting notion, though I suspect Lisa needs to read more comprehensively in the field.

Alone in my room, I laughed out loud. *I suspect so, too,* I typed, when I was able. *Tell you what, I'll go to bed now if you will.*

There was a slight pause, then: *That sounds a fair bargain. Good-night, Jennifer. Sleep well.*

You, too, I typed, and the chat screen shimmered and vanished.

7

I did go to bed, which was the letter of the bargain.

The sheets beneath the quilts were cold. I slid squeamishly between them and lay flat on my back, grimly waiting for my body heat to do its work. Beside me, Jasper stretched, straightening all four legs—and all eighteen claws—in a move so emphatic the bed shook. He relaxed again without waking.

My body finally heated the bed; I drowsed, then woke, crankily aware that *now* I was hot. I twisted around, got even hotter, and finally pitched back the top quilt. Jasper uttered a startled "Mwerp?" and tunneled between the rumbled layers. I heard the solid thump of him hitting the rag rug on the opposite side of the bed.

I pounded on the sides of my pillow and flumped down, arms rigid, hands fisted at my sides, screwed my eyes shut like a little kid pretending to be asleep and lay there, feeling frighteningly close to tears.

I do not cry. My mother had disapproved of tears, as had my father. The White Sheep—my sister, Carol—and I were indoctrinated early, and trained even more closely by the good Sisters at the Roman Catholic elementary school we both attended. The training had been rigorous—perhaps a shade too rigorous—but my life had proven out the basic assertion: Crying does no one any good. Tears are a waste of energy that should be applied to solving the problem.

Tears are despicable. Only excuses are more so.

Back in October, a man had done his best to kill me. There'd been a gun and a murmur of rape—and a generous helping of idiot good luck, the end of it all being that the man was dead and I wasn't, though of course I'd wrecked my car.

But life doesn't stop just because somebody tries to murder you. There'd been chores to tend to, the cat to feed, my job to go to, the insurance company to fight with, a car to buy–and I'd also been raised to tend to my chores. If anyone'd asked me how I was handling the leftovers from the attempt on my life, I'd have said, somewhat blankly, "Oh. Fine."

Because it's easy, when you live alone, when you've always been a night person and a shade on the testy side, to ignore the facts and not admit that bedtime had been creeping later and later into tomorrow morning, and that one's temper was perhaps, just a little, only a bit, shorter–edgier–than was absolutely customary.

And then a kid you don't even know gets herself hit by a car and dead–and your subconscious leaps at the chance to show its wares.

I was cold again, but stubbornly kept flat; tried, in fact, to relax my arms and let the fists ease open.

"Prrt?" The question was simultaneous with a weight hitting the mattress near my right knee. Jasper walked up my hip and stood half on my stomach and half on my chest. I squinted my eyes open and could just make out his face, staring down into mine.

"Prrt," he stated, with emphasis, and neatly lay himself down. He began to purr.

Cautiously, I raised my right hand and rubbed his cheek. The purrs intensified.

I fell asleep with my hand tucked flat against his side.

*

Jasper departed abruptly at five-thirty, all four feet pushing against my chest with surprising force.

"Hey!"

Thump. Which was the cat hitting the floor, then nothing, which in all likelihood was the cat sauntering out of the bedroom and down the hall.

I took a few experimental breaths, decided that my breastbone was not crushed, but that the short jolt of adrenaline had been sufficient to banish any desire to sleep.

Well, wasn't early rising a virtue? I flung back the covers and rose into the shiverful predawn, found jeans, thick socks and a heavy wool pullover by a process composed of equal parts touch and telepathy, then headed for the kitchen to make coffee.

The last drop was dripping when I heard the familiar bang, clatter and clunk that signaled Harry Pelletier's ratty pickup was negotiating my driveway.

"Company," I told Jasper, who was eating breakfast. He flicked his left ear—to acknowledge the receipt of information, I suppose—and continued to chow down while I walked over to the plank door, worked the lock and pulled it open.

"Mornin', mornin'." Harry stumped up onto the porch, and held out a shiny pink-and-white box about the size of a shoe box. "I got the doughnuts, you got the bean?"

"Funny you should ask," I said and stepped back to let her in.

Haroldene Pelletier had been my aunt Jennifer's best friend. She's a blocky, gap-toothed woman in her sixties, and this morning her shoulder-length gray hair was squinched down along the sides of her face by a black woolen watch cap that was snowy with lint.

She stumped across the kitchen in her hard boots and put the box on the kitchen table. Then she stumped over to the pegs set in the wall near the ell, reached up and yanked off the watch cap. Static fizzed and half her hair lifted. She shook the cap out and hung it on a peg, then laboriously shed the red plaid lumberman's jacket, quilted green flannel shirt and thick pink cardigan.

While she was undressing, I poured coffee into two of Aunt Jen's heavy pottery mugs and set them out on the table with a pair of mismatched saucers for doughnut plates. I pulled a carton of milk out of the round-shouldered refrigerator and put it on the table, by which time Harry, looking positively svelte in a brown turtleneck, cranberry colored corduroy shirt and heavy-duty dungarees, had joined me.

"Up early," she observed, pulling the box forward and breaking the sealing tape with a hard thumbnail.

"Bad night for sleeping," I said and poured milk in my coffee. Harry extracted a filled doughnut from the box. A twist of pink icing decorated one end. She cocked a eye at me.

"Saw where that young girl died," she said, which is not at all surprising.

Maine is a hard-scrabble state, no matter what the tourism department or the city folks in Portland try to tell you. Haroldene Pelletier is no different than her neighbors. She brings the ends that never do quite meet a bit closer together by swapping goods and services, and works odd jobs to keep the cash trickling in.

In the winter, her list of odd jobs includes delivering the *Wimsy Voice*. Summertime, the route belongs to Stephen Thiebolt, who delivered year-round for twenty-five years, until the winters began to wear on him. Now he leases the route to Harry from November first through the end of Mud–which is called April in the rest of the country–while he lives the high life in a three-room trailer in a park in Gainesville, Florida.

Harry took a bite of her sweet, then put it on the saucer while she stirred two spoonsful of sugar into her black coffee.

"Hell of a winter," she commented, somewhat indistinctly. "Already cold enough to freeze the titties off a bull and we ain't come to Christmas yet." She sighed and took a swig of coffee. "Heater went bust on the truck."

And her out during the coldest hours, delivering the paper along the back roads of Wimsy.

"Better get it fixed," I said, and raised my mug. I gave her what I hoped was a stern stare over the rim. "I mean it, Harry. You'll freeze to death out there at three a.m. in a truck with no heater."

"Oh, I'll get 'er patched," she said. "Dubois owes me."

Jakey Dubois is a mechanic-without-portfolio. He owns his tools and keeps his General Motors Automotive School certificate in a clear plastic envelope in the bottom of his toolbox. He does not own a garage, preferring to travel to the homes of his customers and doctor their vehicles in dooryard or driveway, but he can cadge lift or garage space from any of the established shops in Wimsy, Waterville or Winslow, should the patient require hospitalization.

"Call him when you get home," I said. "If he can't fix it today, call me and I'll let you use my car tonight."

Doughnut halfway to her mouth, Harry laughed.

"Sure you will! What a sight I'd be in that rig of yours, slung so low my ass'll be frostbit from sitting on the ground— besides not being able to reach up to the paper boxes."

I grinned, reluctantly. "Well, if he can't fix it today, then maybe you can borrow Morris' truck this evening."

Morris DuChamp owns Old Smokey Orchards on the other side of the Point and is another of my aunt's old friends. He and Harry have been amicably feuding for approximately my entire lifetime.

"That's all right, we'll get it solved," Harry said, and took another bite of her doughnut. She chewed, swallowed and used the bit-off end as a pointer, stabbing first in my direction, then toward the breached pastry box.

"Whole dozen of them doughnuts in there," she told me. "Hope you don't think I'm gonna eat 'em all."

"I'm not real hungry right now, thanks."

"Trouble with you, you're never real hungry," Harry said, slipping easily into one of her favorite topics. "Girl your age needs some meat on her bones."

"I'm thirty-five years old."

"What I said." She nodded, finished her doughnut in two bites and chugged coffee. I sipped from my own mug and tried not to be annoyed.

In Baltimore, a city that idolized the icon of the slender, vital businesswoman, I was a shade too tall, a touch too thin. Blame it on a steady diet of caffeine and a general disinterest in foodstuffs. The story might have been different if I'd ever learned to cook, but my mother's notion of high cuisine–dry roast beef, lumpy mashed potatoes and canned peas boiled to mush–had done little to incline me toward the art.

In Maine, where baked beans is a breakfast food and that same breakfast is more often than not rounded out with a doughnut and second cup of coffee, the ideal is a shorter, sturdier build, more adapted to dealing with winter's frigid fun days.

"I'm a racehorse in a stable full of Percherons," I said, finishing off my coffee and putting the mug down with a slight thump. "I'm unappreciated."

Harry paused with her hand in the doughnut box, giving me a considering look out of round blue eyes.

"Race horse slips on the ice out there this morning, she'll break all four legs," she said. "I ain't saying these are as heavy as some, but one doughnut could make the difference."

I grinned, stood, picked up her mug and mine.

"More coffee?"

"Yessir."

I went over to the counter, refilled the mugs, coincidentally emptying the coffeepot, came back and put Harry's by her right hand, sat down in my place–and found myself staring into the depths of the pink-and-white box.

Oh, what the hell.

I hauled out a glazed doughnut and put in on my saucer.

"Plans for the day?" Harry asked, sugaring her mug.

I broke my doughnut and dunked half of it, taking a sweet, soggy bite before turning my head to consult the calendar hanging on the wall over Communications Central.

"Today is Monday the twelfth," I said, mentally reviewing my work schedule.

"I've got an interview at two . . ." I sighed and shook

my head, for the first time fully accepting the necessity. After all, if Fox was willing to don a tuxedo, my sacrifice could justly be no less than his.

"Guess I'm going to buy a party dress," I told Harry, and dunked my doughnut again.

8

The Cinderella Shoppe had for several generations been owned and operated by the Dostie family. A year ago, plagued by ill health and harboring the strong and possibly subversive conviction that somewhere it must be *warm*, Sylvia Dostie, last of her line, had put the business up for sale.

It was purchased almost immediately by one Eustacie Parmentier, a shiny new graduate of the Fine Arts program at Colby College. This is called "buying a job," and in Central Maine it's fast becoming the only way to get hired.

Having purchased her job, Eustacie–known to her friends as "Mike"–went to with a will. She hung new awnings, dumped the Willendorf plaster mannequins in favor of a modest grouping of four smoked Lucite female shapes, glitzed up the display window and extended the Shoppe's open hours to include Friday evening and Saturday afternoon.

Change is highly suspect in the greater Wimsy area. Initial reaction to Mike's alterations to what was, after all, a Community Mainstay was not positive. But Mike was not only canny, she had staying power.

She bought the business in February, made the majority of her changes throughout March. By that time, the various proms and promettes of what Maine considers to be spring could be seen hovering in the wings and what self-respecting darling of any mother's heart would dare appear in a gown from J.C. Penney's?

Besides Penney's (or *homemade*), Mike was the only game in several towns. Fashion hunger overcame outrage and the Cinderella Shoppe sold dozens of prom gowns, followed by scores of wedding gowns and bridesmaid's dresses.

The premier wedding season ends in mid-October,

because even in Maine there are optimists, and the fancy dress business settled down a bit, leaving Mike free to pore over fashion industry papers and line catalogs, making Cinderella's wish list for next year.

Which is what she was doing when I walked in.

A bell chimed gently as I opened the door, repeating its two note message when I closed it. The Shoppe was lit by overhead fluorescents, sun-bright after the frigid gloom of mid-morning. Mike was sitting at a white and gold spider-leg desk situated near the fitting room, and commanding a clear view of the door. Her head was bent over a magazine page; wet-looking puddles of color gleaming under the beam of her desk lamp.

I'd drawn the story when Mike first bought the business. She glanced up now with a slight frown, then grinned in recognition.

"Hey, the press! Slow news week?"

"About normal, for the beginning of hibernation season."

She laughed and pushed back from the desk, shaking her hair out of her eyes and standing.

Mike is what most times passes for tall in a woman—five-seven, maybe five-eight. Her shoulder-length naturally dark brown hair is locked in a constant, to-the-death struggle with Miss Clairol Chestnut Surprise Rinse for Your Hair. She wears huge round glasses rimmed in red tortoiseshell. The top hemisphere of each lens is tinted the same lightish brown as her eyes, the bottom halves are pink. Being a Fine Arts graduate, she wears a lot of black—straight skirts and straight tops, with two or more scarves floating at more-or-less shoulder-height, and a severe lack of jewelry.

Her own choice of mode aside, she also has the finest eye for *fit* in the larger Central Maine region.

"I need help," I told her.

Mike stretched her arms wide. "Ask."

I reached into my pocketbook, pulled out The Twins'

invitation and passed it over.

"Yummy," she said, giving the card a quick, competent glance before handing it back. "You need a dress, yes?"

"I need a dress, yes."

"So, you come to zee right plaze," she said, hamming it. She spun on her toes, arms outstretched again to show me the glittering racks of improbable clothing. "What we have, eez dresses."

"There's a slight problem," I said apologetically, as she spun back to face me. She lifted haughty eyebrows behind her tinted eyewear.

"And that would be?"

"Myself," I confessed, and sighed, looking around at the tissue-glitter, low-cut confections. Carly could wear any one of these items at random, and look seductively lush. I glanced back to Mike. "No cleavage. Too tall. Too skinny. I'd look like Barbie's vampire roommate in one of those things."

"Hmm." Her face turned serious. She looked me up. She looked me down.

"Take your coat off."

I did. She took it and laid it across her desk, then walked around me, taking her time about it. I stood still and tried not to feel utterly awkward.

Mike completed her circuit.

"You're right," she said, crossing her arms under her breasts. Light from the overheads glazed her lenses into a pinkish brown mirror, hiding her eyes.

"These dresses are for the common run," Mike said, and grinned at me. "For you, something–" She kissed the tips of her fingers and tossed the kiss toward the ceiling, "*different.*"

"Something cheap?" I asked, not too hopefully. Mike shrugged the question away with the contempt it deserved.

"We can go long skirt–full, with lots of gold and sable and sapphire . . . For the top, something high-necked and authoritative in black–a smatter of jewelry. I know I have something . . ." She caught my arm and steered me to the dressing room. "I'll bring it," she said, and left me.

She was back before I'd finished shaking the static out of my pullover, hanging skirt and top on wall hooks before whisking away again.

I fingered the skirt, which looked like a patchwork quilt as sewn by the lady of the castle, from squares of her worn out velvets and gold-shot satins. I touched the high-necked authoritative black top—Lycra, the wonder fabric. Eventually, I divested, vested and stepped out into the Shoppe, where Mike and the tri-fold mirror were waiting.

I did look formal, that much was certain. The patchwork skirt had a lovely weight to it and rustled when I moved. The lycra-woven top did its magic, molding and holding what there was to either. I looked in the mirror and felt, just slightly– dismayed.

I look like Aunt Sara from England, I complained to myself. Myself sighed and pointed out that aloof elegance was about the best affect the physical plant was capable of producing and who was I trying to impress, anyway?

"Wait a sec," said Mike from behind my shoulder. "I just thought of something else."

I went back into the dressing room and divested once again. In due time, Mike reappeared. I donned the garment she brought me–

And stood staring at the reflection in the dressing room's single mirror. After a full minute, I shook myself and went out to the tri-fold.

The dress was rough-finished off-white satin. Three small satin frogs fastened the high neck along one side and down to the right shoulder. Long, tight, sleeves. The rest of the dress was merely a long sheath, with a shape that hugged mine so faithfully that it would have been impossible to walk without the left-side hem-to-mid-thigh slit.

I stood in the middle of the tri-fold and stared.

"Well?" Mike asked, behind me.

I turned to look at her, though I still reserved an edge

of my eye for my reflection.

"Who is this woman and why have I never seen her before?" I demanded.

Mike grinned. "It's you," she announced, which it patently was not, but why argue? She rubbed her palms together. "It's on sale, too."

*

I had to go over to Waterville to buy the off-white satin pumps to match the dress. While I was on that side of the river, I used my Penney's credit card to pick up the various underpinnings recommended by Mike, swept by McD's for a lunch of fishburger and coffee, and made my two o'clock interview with whole seconds to spare.

The hands on the newsroom clock were creeping up on four when I walked in the side door, having virtuously stopped for the early cop log after my interview.

Dayside–also known as "Features" or, according to Bill Jacques, "The Ladies Aid and Social Society"–was quiet, which was odd. Four o'clock was well into the late-afternoon kaffeeklatsch and gossip hour. I craned my neck to see over the movable partition that separated Us from Them and saw the three women who made up Features studiously at their machines.

Odder and odder.

I cut through Sports, waving at Jack-the-Jock and Kevin and receiving polite return waves, but no boisterous invitation to buy into the football pool, which I never did and which never once stopped Jack from asking.

Maybe there was a flu going 'round, I speculated, then stepped into the main aisle, whereupon speculation ceased.

Standing directly before Bill Jacques' desk. Indeed, *looming over* Bill Jacques, his computer and all that kingdom that was Bill's own. Standing there, cashmere-sweater-clad, the blank pages of tomorrow's paper shuffling between them like a bad juggling act while they muttered to each other, but not to Bill, were John and Jerry Talbot. The Twins. Jay-Two, Tee-Two.

The owners. Our—not to put too fine a point on it—bosses.

No wonder everybody looked so happy.

There is a line from the sainted and revered *Fiddler on the Roof* in which the Rabbi calls upon God to "bless and keep the Czar—far away from us." I believe it not unfair to state that majority of the *Voice*'s employees feel just this way with regard to The Twins. Nor do I believe it is inaccurate to say that The Twins return the warmth of their employees' regard, in every shaded nuance.

Don't get me wrong. The Twins aren't bad men. It is true that they're spoiled, egocentric and rude, but they possesses true democratic spirit. They treat *everybody* like the neighbor's dog. The trick is to not take it personally.

It's not a trick I've quite caught onto, myself.

I took a careful breath and went down the Twin-choked aisle, heading for my desk.

"Excuse me," I murmured, hoping that they were so involved in their muttering and second-guessing that they'd simply shift without looking up.

No such luck.

One of them—I think it was Jerry, but The Twins are identicals and I don't really see them often enough to be able to say which is who with any degree of certainty—glanced up, frowning all over his smooth-shaven tennis-tanned face.

"What shift are you working?" he barked.

This was gratifying, in its way. At least he remembered that I worked here.

"Two to eight," I said, holding my eyebrows level by an act of sheer willpower.

"*Two* to eight," he repeated, with emphasis, and made a show of glancing downroom to the newsroom clock before looking back to me, *his* eyebrows up as high as they would go.

I grit my teeth and deliberately did not look at Bill Jacques.

"I had an interview at two o'clock, which lasted to three-fifteen. On my way back, I stopped at the cop shop to pick up the log. It's on the sheet." I stared at him for a moment, feeling my temper creeping toward *flare*, and when he showed no willingness to move *yet*, said, flatly, "You're in my way."

He blinked.

"I still don't know about this front page, Jer," his brother said, shuffling papers again. "What do you think about moving . . ."

In the Mystic Game of Life, as played by the Talbot Twins, there is a much higher percentage attached to yanking Bill Jacques' leash than in punching my buttons. Jerry turned back to his brother, moving a millimeter or so in toward the half-wall, to let me by.

I grit my teeth, started to slither past and felt my temper go from *flare* to *fuck this*.

"Mr. Talbot, please move!" I stated, in my best "all-right-now-boys-and-girls" voice.

Both Mr. Talbots started, heads jerking in my direction amid a clatter of papers.

"Well," said Jerry, covering his startlement. "Ex-cuuuuse us." He made a show of flattening himself against the half-wall and reached out to pull his brother back, too.

"After *you*, Ms. Pierce," John invited, waving tomorrow's dummy pages like a flag.

"Thank you," I said calmly, and walked, did not run, past them and down to my desk.

*

The shift was a nightmare, of course. The shift was always a nightmare when The Twins were involved.

They changed the layout of the front page three times, dealing stories like card tricks. They rewrote every one of Bill

Jacques' headlines, second-guessed his sizing and had Dan Skat back to the darkroom four times for "a little burn on this one," "bring this *up*, dammit!" and other so-called improvements.

John and Jerry Talbot are not newspapermen. They do not live in Wimsy, Maine, and tend to find the residents thereof—as they tend to find their employees—slightly ridiculous and not a little stupid. Their main interest in the *Voice* is as a source of money. And when they're in town, they like to play.

So John and Jerry played and Bill Jacques got redder and more taciturn and the shift ran long and when I finally escaped, at ten-fifteen, I had a pounding headache.

At home, I hung the parka on its peg and leaned my forehead against the wall, taking deep, supposedly calming breaths. This exercise was interrupted by a bump against the back of my legs, which was Jasper, saying hi and politely requesting attention to his food dish.

I fed him, took three aspirin and carried a glass of wine upstairs with me to the computer room.

There was mail waiting on the Net. I downloaded it and hesitated with my hand on the mouse, trying to decide if I was feeling patient enough to visit a chat salon. I wasn't.

I logged off and dialed *Random Access.*

The first message in the Speakeasy was from Lisa.

You know how they say bad things come in threes? And it's true—I hurt my hands and lost my job and then Dan left. But I think it's the same with good things, that they come in threes, too. Because look I got a job and today I got a phone call from Dan and he's coming home. He says he was wrong, that we can make it work, we've just got to talk to each other—and I think that it would be great, after he's settled and all, if I got pregnant right away and then we could be our own family and—

The words broke apart and a moment later I was facing not Lisa's hosannas but the familiar bisected blue screen.

Good evening, Jennifer.

I smiled, as if he could see me through the screen.

Hi. I hope your day's been better than mine.

It's been tolerable, Fox allowed. *I've gotten almost half of those stupid machines up to spec. Carl should have the parts he ordered for me tomorrow and with a little luck the whole police station should be networked by this time next week.*

Hooray for the good guys, I typed, and then: *The Twins are at the paper. Last I saw they were making Bill Jacques' life a burden and a misery.*

There was a momentary pause. *I'll call him.*

It looked like it was shaping up to a late night, I demurred.

In that case, I'll meet him for breakfast. What do you think of Lisa's news?

Alone in my room, I sighed and rubbed my forehead. *I hope it works out for her,* I typed slowly, and stopped.

But, prompted Fox after a couple seconds had gone by and I hadn't gotten it together to type anything else.

But, I don't think it will. And then she'll not only be by herself, she'll be by herself and the sole support of an infant. I sighed again, sharply, and wished I wasn't feeling so–tired.

They might make it work, Fox pointed out gently. *Some people do manage it.*

I know, I typed. *I'm pretty zoned. Think I'll call it a night and look for my rose-colored glasses tomorrow.*

All right, said Fox. *Good-night, Jennifer. Sleep well.*

You, too, I returned, my hand moving toward the disconnect. I hesitated. My fingers took advantage of the pause to tap out three quick letters on the keyboard.

Fox.

Yes?

Thank you, my fingers typed, while I watched and wondered what they were going to say next.

But unspecified gratitude appeared to be all that my fingers wished to convey on my behalf this evening.

On Fox's end, there was hesitation, then: *You're*

*welcome. And thank you. Go to sleep, Jennifer. I'll talk with
you tomorrow.*

    Right, I said. *Good-night.*

    I didn't have to hit the disconnect. Fox took charge
from his side and logged me off.

    In my room, I finished my wine, shut down the machine
and went to bed. In spite of it all, I slept straight through to
morning, without dreams.

9

The phone rang at 8 a.m.

The list of people who will call me at 8 a.m. is: Harry Pelletier, but try calling *her* at midnight; Barbara Doolittle, because she is a faerie creature, above the considerations of mere time and space; and, very rarely and only because she needs to, Marian Younger.

I managed to get an arm out from beneath the quilt and snatched up the receiver before the second ring had quite died away.

"Morning," I told it—not quite a mumble.

"And so it *is* morning, you *clever* girl!" Trilling.

Not Harry, calling with a broken down truck and five miles of newspapers to be delivered. Not Marian, calling for a ride because the school district had forgotten—again—to send the bus with the chairlift. Trilling. At 8 a.m. I resisted the impulse to hang up.

"Hi, Barbara."

"Good-morning, sweetheart," she cooed. "I didn't *wake* you, did I?" She knew better than to pause there and swept on without taking a breath. "Jendarling, I *just* finished reading your piece for next time and it's brilliant, sweetheart, *positively* brilliant." This was pure softener, had nothing to do with truth as we know it, and is most generally found followed by a 'but.'

"But," Barbara continued, "there's just a *teensy* little problem—nothing *horrid*, sweetheart, but you know we have to be *perfectly* explicit even over the silliest things for our readership."

Our readership is actually a pretty fair portion of the Rest of the Country. The magazine of which Barbara Doolittle is editor-in-chief is *Maine Life*, a four-color photo-glutted, digest-sized bimonthly magazine designed to exhibit Maine Quaintness to those unfortunate enough to live somewhere else.

Maine Life does not ask the hard questions, and investigative reporting is absolutely taboo. Barbara wants feel-good feature stories about Maine people, places and things, always bearing in mind that there can be no *ugliness* attached to any *Maine Life* story. Quaintness is all.

It is a sad fact that Maine Quaintness sells well, beyond the borders. *Maine Life* does nicely, thank you, and pays handsomely.

I've been one of Barbara's army of freelancers for a little under a year. "Next time" was the January/February issue, for which I'd submitted a historical piece on Richmond's Ferry, which plied the Smoke from Wimsy to Waterville and back again from 1798 straight through to September 30, 1953. I'd worked hard on the story, spent hours in the Wimsy Historical Society, paging through the old log books; carefully going through cracking photographs, talking with the curator–and most especially with those Wimsy residents who remembered riding the ferry.

I'd worked hard and I'd been proud of the story when I turned it in.

And now there was a *teensy* problem. I grit my teeth to keep the sigh back and pushed upright against my pillows, cradling the receiver between shoulder and cheek while I groped on the night stand for the pad and pen I kept there.

"OK," I said to Barbara. "What needs repair?"

"Sweetheart, so *gruff*," Barbara chided, and proceeded, at length, to tell me.

*

The revisions weren't horrible. Not exactly horrible. In fact, I had most of what I needed in my notes and garnered the last bit of missing clarity in a quick phone call to Mildred

Begin, the curator of the Wimsy Historical Society. It only remained to fit the new information seamlessly into the existing story.

I am not a writer by training, though I am a life member of the Voracious Readers Society. Reporters, understand, are not writers. Reporters go, they see, they ask a few questions and then they tell the folks at home what they saw and heard. Think of the messenger in the Book of Job: *And I am escaped alone to tell thee.* It's a craft that demands clarity, but not much art.

The work I do for *Maine Life* does demand art and I sweat each sentence, turning and polishing, dismantling, remantling and polishing some more, until I'm satisfied that what I have is as near to perfect as I'm capable of producing. This time.

Viewed this way, the Richmond's Ferry retrospective was the best thing I'd written in my young career. I was annoyed that I hadn't been smart enough to see and fill the holes Barbara had identified during the initial writing and afraid that I was going to ruin the piece by the ineptness of my patch job.

I started patching at nine. At one, I had a final version that the perfectionist living in my head allowed "would do." While it was printing, I dashed into the bathroom for the world-famous eighty-second shower, dried my hair with the blower on "supermax," leapt into a pair of jeans and the first sweater that came to hand.

Back in my office, I addressed a manila envelope, put the revised story inside, sealed it and ran downstairs, narrowly avoiding tripping on Jasper, who was lying, log-like, against the riser of the third stair from the top.

In the kitchen, I paused long enough to yank on, but not zip, the purple parka, snatch up my purse and flee down the ell to the barn.

I parked in the municipal lot next to the Wimsy Police Station, ran across the street to the post office and sent the manuscript on its way to Portland, where Barbara–God bless

the United States Postal System within the state of Maine—
would receive it tomorrow morning.

It was quarter to two when I left the post office, which
meant I was early for my shift. Feeling virtuous, if a little
winded, I pulled my notebook out of my pocket and went
across to the police station to pick up the early log.

*

Ken Aube was standing at the dispatcher's desk, holding
a five-and-a-quarter inch floppy disk. The disk was not in a
protective sleeve and bore no label that I could see. Ken was
holding it by one corner, jiggling it absently while he talked to
the dispatcher.

"Damn kids—what're they going to get into next?" He
shook his head and jiggled the disk harder. "A virus. How am
I supposed to check and see if this thing has a virus on it?
And what if there is? No law against carrying a virus in your
pocket, if you want to."

"There's a law against malicious mischief," I said, as
the gate banged closed behind me.

"Well, that's true," Ken allowed. "But it's not malicious
just sitting here on the disk. If somebody uses it deliberately
to make a computer sick, then we get into malicious mischief."
He sighed. "I guess."

I grinned and nodded at the disk still jiggling in his
hand. "Where'd you get it?"

"One of the no-trouble kids from the high school
brought it in. Claims there's a virus on it and that a couple of
the—less desirables—were planning on making all the computers
in the lab sick with it." He sighed down at the disk, and skated
it across the room to his desk, where it came to rest against the
Big Apple coffee mug.

"Kids."

I frowned, because I'd lost a hard drive and all the files
and programs on it to a particularly virulent computer virus

early in my modeming career and am inclined to take these matters seriously. Ken must have caught the frown; he smiled and raised his hands.

"I'll go on up and talk with the computer teacher," he said. "What else can you do?"

"It's just that viruses really can do damage," I said, earnestly. "Trash a machine and make it unusable. If the high school lost the computer lab . . ."

"Wouldn't be pretty," Ken agreed. "I'll do my duty, Jen, don't worry."

He grinned and sauntered away, toward the back room and his desk. The dispatcher shoved the log toward me and I flipped pages, copying down the three new entries, unsurprised but curiously saddened to find Jimmy Danforth's name: Shoplifting at the IGA.

Last entry copied, I straightened and took a look around me, belatedly noticing the lack of clutter.

"What happened to all the boxes?" I asked the dispatcher.

He shrugged. "Computer guy took 'em out to work on 'em," he said without much interest. "Said he needed room."

I nodded. "Guess things'll be a lot easier, once the new network's installed."

He shrugged again. "Don't know what we need it for," he said, echoing of Ken Aube's sentiments. "Done fine without this long."

There didn't seem to be much to say to that, so I nodded good-bye and headed out, tucking the notebook into my pocket as I went.

*

Back at the newsroom, I checked the roster, noting that my three o'clock chat with the Code Enforcement Officer had been rescheduled for four, then went to my desk, fired up the computer and transcribed the meager cop log. That chore out of the way, I turned my attention to the pile of news briefs waiting to be input.

In the misty past, before the advent of The Twins and cost-cutting measures, the *Voice* had employed a brace of typesetters, whose function it was to input community notes, news shorts, obits and letters to the editor while answering the phone and acting as newsroom receptionists.

The Twins had halved the compliment of typesetters and failed to replace the second when she quit a couple months later, citing overwork. The inputting of press releases, etc., was then divided equally between the three reporters. I tried to devote at least a half-hour to my stack every shift, which, since I'm a professionally trained ten-finger touch typist, keeps me pretty well abreast of my obligation. Sue Danforth picks hers out at thirty painful words a minute and sometimes stays overshift to finish. Milt types his share when forced to it by editorial threats. When the pile on his desk gets too high, I've seen him take a handful of pages from the bottom and surreptitiously slide them into his trash can.

I opened a file in my computer, titled it "Brfs12.13", pulled the stack into comfortable reading distance and began to type.

I like to type: the faster, the better. It's a kind of Zen, where the words flow from the page through your eyes, down your arm, into your fingers, which flick them into the computer. On a good day, the effect is of whipping, dreamlike speed. On a good day, I can clock a hundred—a hundred-twenty—words a minute.

This was a good day. In less than two minutes I was whipping along at ninety-plus, hazed in that perfection of mindful mindlessness so dear to the Zen master's heart, lost to my surroundings, at one with my task.

"Now that's fast!" The voice was admiring, female, strongly Southern. My fingers staggered on the keys as I jumped, eyes breaking contact with the page as I looked up.

The population of Central Maine is largely Caucasian,

with a smattering of American Indian. The woman before me was chocolate-skinned, fortyish and dressed for the executive suite of a major corporation. Her jewelry was gold and expensively subdued, her suit tailored out of garnet-colored wool.

The hand she raised to soothe me was ringless, smooth and manicured.

"There, now, I didn't mean to startle you," she said, smiling. She moved her hand forward, across the top of the computer. "Serena Jefferson."

"Jennifer Pierce." We shook. Her hand was cold and dry.

"Now, are you the typesetter?" She asked, tipping her head and smiling again. It would have been a nicer smile if it had made it to her eyes; as it was, it fit seamlessly with the rest of her tailored, expensive look.

"I'm one of the reporters," I said. "The paper doesn't employ typesetters at the moment."

"It doesn't," she said, the warm Southern voice flattening a little, then coming back, full tilt. "Well, I am amazed. I haven't seen anyone type like that for–it must be twenty years. I'm happy to see it's not a lost art."

"Not quite lost," I said, treating her to one of my politest secretarial smiles. "Is there something I can do for you?" I suggested. "Perhaps you're here to see Mr. Jacques . . . ?"

"Oh, my . . ." She put her hand on her breast and gave a breathy little laugh. "I thank you, but I'm with the rest of the survey group. Just got a little ahead of Mr. Talbot, I guess . . ."

As if on cue, I heard voices in the hall. A moment later, The Twins entered the newsroom down by Features, leading a be-suited tour group of three men and a woman.

"I'll just rejoin them now," said Serena Jefferson and smiled again. "A pleasure to meet you, Ms. Pierce." She turned and was gone before I could return the compliment.

The Twins ushered their group past the movable wall

and into Features, Serena Jefferson slipping after them a moment later, while I sat behind my computer, blinking like an idiot, Zen in pieces all about.

    Survey team?

10

Friday dawned jewel-like: A brilliant, windless winter day, with the temperature hovering at just-about-twenty-five. Above zero.

I drank my second cup of coffee standing by Communications Central, gazing out the window at the bird feeder. We had the usual crowd this morning: chickadees, gold and purple finches, a handful of house sparrows. Every so often a blue jay would descend, shrieking invective and scattering the smaller birds; at which point Jasper, who was sitting in the window watching the show with intensity, would hunch down, lay his ears back and emit a sound closely resembling "MakmakMAK-makmak!" The jay, gobbling sunflower seeds from the feeder with the chutzpah of a party-guest picking cashews out of the mixed nut dish, ignored him.

Coffee done, I tackled the house chores–a little dusting, a little vacuuming, a couple loads of laundry–the usual Friday routine. I made a grilled cheese sandwich for lunch, washed it down with a tall glass of orange juice, did the dishes, refilled the bird feeder from the dwindling seed supply and set out for town.

At Dore's Hardware I lugged fifty pounds of bird seed in two twenty-five-pound bags–at one trip per bag–to the counter, ignoring the minor kvetching from the shoulder I'd damaged in a car crash five years ago.

"Cheaper if you buy the fifty-pounder," Alvie Dore told me, hand poised over cash register keys.

I nodded. "Problem is, I can't carry the fifty-pounder."

"Ayuh, there's a problem," Alvie agreed, but didn't punch in the purchase even then. Instead, he put his hands flat on the counter, one on either side of the cash register, and looked from me to the bags and back again.

"In a hurry for those?" he asked eventually.

I blinked at him.

"What I mean is," he said, "Julie's for the Galen girl's birthday party tomorrow afternoon. Won't take him a minute to swing down the Point and drop you off fifty pound. You just tell him where you want it set down."

Julie is Julian Dore, sixteen years old and Alvie's youngest. I blinked again.

"I don't want to put him out—" I started.

"Won't be," Alvie assured me, and finally moved, punching the sale into the register. "That's ten-twenty-three," which was the lower, one-bag price. He nodded at the twenty-five-pounders beached on the counter. "Don't worry about those. I'll put 'em back."

"Thank you," I said cautiously, handing him a ten and a quarter.

"You betcha." He rang the drawer open and passed over my two cents. I dropped them into the Styrofoam cup next to the register.

"Party's set to start around two," he said as I slipped my wallet away. "You'll see Julie about quarter-of, I'd say."

"Thank you," I said again. Alvie nodded and reached over to the abandoned bird seed. Still feeling a little dazed, I went out into the brilliant cold.

Next stop was the CPU, for a box of disks and a quick look around. I shook myself and headed up Main Street.

The Central Processing Unit is a triangular building set into the corner of Main and Preble opposite Karen's Kraft Korner. The door faces the intersection of the two streets, and is flanked by two curving show windows. The site had formerly housed a Sears Catalog Sales store.

The door announced me with an electronic "ding-ding" loud enough to reach Carl in the backest corner of the storeroom—necessary, as Carl usually runs the shop single-handed. This does not, however, mean that the CPU is *empty*.

It also serves as a sort of impromptu clubhouse for Wimsy's harder core computerist population, often harboring two to six hangers-on, most of whom know the stock as well as Carl and are perfectly willing to talk for hours about the benefits of the Pentium 90 motherboard, say, over a 486/1000.

This afternoon, the retinue was two. Doug Nolan waved with one hand from the front work table while popping a disk into the machine in front of him and tapping the enter key with the other hand. Loading software, I thought with a grin. Carl wasn't above pressing the CPU's hangers-on into labor from time to time.

The second denizen was seated at a work table by the door to the so-called Tech Support Area, which is where Carl does the internal repairs and rebuildings too bloody to be displayed before the eyes of the public. It is, in fact, unusual to see a machine without its case outside of Tech Support, though it does sometimes happen. Like today.

I walked quietly toward the back, where Marian was working on the innards of a desk-top CPU, tiny screwdriver steady in her hand, face scrunched up in concentration, her wheelchair pulled up as close to the table as possible.

Marian Younger is not one of the regular hangers-on at Carl's. In fact, Marian is most usually in one of two places—school, or the suite of rooms allotted to her on the second floor of her parents' house, where she amuses herself by listening to the police scanner, reading, building and repairing computers and other small electric devices, and calling electronic bulletin boards from one end of the country to the other and, for all I know, on other planets, too.

I met Marian on a bulletin board—a weird little net out of Memphis called *Creature Feature*—and we'd chatted for months before realizing that we not only lived in the same state, but in the same *town*.

Board finally seated to her satisfaction, Marian put the 'driver down and looked up.

"Hi, Jen." She didn't seem particularly surprised to

see me, but it takes an event of epic significance to rattle the mantle of chilly calm Marian habitually wears.

"Hi," I said, pointing at the naked machine before her. "Got a job?"

She nodded seriously. "Sub-contractor. Fox and Carl find which boards are bust or missing. I do the installation, then they go back into the tech room for testing and burn-in."

"Sounds like a system. This the police station network?"

Another nod. "Fox says he wants it out of his hair by the end of next week."

I grinned. "Fox is an optimist."

"I never considered optimism one of my failings," commented a light, familiar voice, "but I fear you're correct. This job will simply go on and on, stretching out into my twilight years, to eventually be listed as a non sequitur in the inventory of my estate."

I laughed. Fox, leaning against the door frame of Tech Support, gave one of his slight smiles.

"A non sequitur?" I demanded.

"What would you call it?" he returned, crossing his arms over his chest. He was wearing an old flannel shirt in blue-and-white plaid, sleeves rolled halfway to the elbow, and a pair of comfortably faded jeans.

"How about a disaster?"

"Oh, no, it's not nearly a disaster." He tipped his head, as if giving the point consideration. "At least, not yet."

"Might as well just call it a comedy of errors an' hope they catch that fella sold 'em all these stupid machines." That was Carl, squeezing past Fox on his way out of Tech Support. He gave me a nod. "Afternoon, Jen. You don't see what you need, sing out, OK?"

"All I need is a box of high density three-and-halfs," I told him and he nodded again before passing on toward the front of the store and Doug Nolan.

"You got that stuff loaded? Man's due in at four . . ."

"Ready for another?" Fox asked Marian.

She shook her head. "I'm not sure about this one wire—seemed like it might be broken in the sheath . . ."

"That won't do, will it?" He came away from his lean and moved to the table, fishing the gold-rimmed glasses out of his breast pocket and flicking them open. "Show me which one."

She pointed and he bent down, one hand braced on the back of the wheelchair, bright head bent above her dark one.

"Aha," he said eventually, straightening and whisking his glasses away. "We shall have recourse to the soldering iron."

"OK," Marian said, settling back. "I can . . ."

"I should have said," Fox murmured apologetically, "that *I* shall have recourse to the soldering iron."

Marian frowned. "I do soldering repairs at home," she informed him, with more than a nip of icy authority.

Fox raised an eyebrow. "I do wish you wouldn't."

The frown this time was glacial. "Why not?"

"Well, for one thing, because you don't have a fire extinguisher in that room, which is very foolish of you, Marian. Electricity is *not* your friend. It is an unpredictable, sometimes deadly force of nature and it should be treated with more respect than you will probably ever accord it, but try anyway."

Marian blinked up at him, mouth slightly open.

"As for soldering up there—" he shook his head, looking even graver than usual.

Marian swallowed and bit her bottom lip. "Stupid, right?"

"Not to put too fine a point on it," Fox agreed. "After all, it's not only yourself you need to consider. Your parents live in the house, too. What if there were an accident—a fire?"

Marian sighed. "Stupid," she decided and glanced over. "Jen?"

"Yo."

"Will you buy me a fire extinguisher, please? I'll—"

"No need to run Jennifer all over town," Fox interrupted, bending down to pick up the machine. "We can make a detour on the way to taking you home and buy a couple. All right?"

She looked back at him, a smile tugging at the corners of her hard, grown-up mouth. "All right," she said. "Thanks."

"You're welcome." He vanished into Tech Support, machine under one arm.

"Here you go," Carl's growl was at my elbow. "One box of high density three-and-a-halfs."

"Thanks," I said, fishing my wallet out. "See you later," I said to Marian. She nodded and raised a hand.

I followed Carl to the cash register. Carl is about six inches shorter than me, broad-shouldered and beer-bellied. His hair hangs below his ears in shaggy gray ringlets; his beard and mustache are snow white. The portions of his face that can be glimpsed through the rug are deeply tanned, soft and wrinkled like an old paper bag.

I gave him a ten; he gave me change and my box. I dropped it into my pocketbook with my wallet and turned to go, nearly falling over Fox in the process.

"Pick you up at seven?" he asked, walking with me toward the door.

I looked at him. "You're going through with it?"

He lifted an eyebrow. "Aren't you?"

"Honor demands no less," I told him and he nodded gravely.

"Precisely. Seven?"

I grinned. "Nothing in Wimsy is an hour away from anything. If you pick me up at seven-thirty we'll still be early."

"Seven-thirty it is," he said, opening the door and letting me out into the dwindling sunlight. He smiled. "See you soon." The door swung shut.

Outside, I took a deep breath of knife-sharp air, then headed down Main Street for the last stop of the afternoon.

*

"Frosty the Snowman" was jigging across the airwaves when I stepped into Mainely Manes. I took off the parka, hung it on a hook and walked over to Phillip's station.

"Ah, Ms. Pierce." Phillip hammed a deep salaam. "Punctual as always." He straightened and picked up an apron, eyebrows high. "Surely we just did the bangs?"

"Surely we did," I agreed and grinned at him as I held my hair out of the way. "I'll tell you what the dress looks like, OK?"

Phillip's light brown eyes lit with artistic fervor. "OK," he said, and swirled the apron into place. "Tell."

11

At 7:25 p.m., I gave Phillip's artful French braids a last pat, checked the makeup I had just finished applying, shook my head one last time at the exotically dressed mystery woman in the mirror and went downstairs to wait for 7:30 and Fox.

He didn't arrive at 7:30; nor did he appear at 7:45.

At 7:55, feeling equal parts steamed and dismayed, I shrugged into my parka and went over to the kitchen table to pick up the tiny off-white satin bag sitting there.

I undid the snap and took out my keys, then stood there holding them, listening to myself say that maybe I ought to really call Fox before I left, that maybe something had gone . . . wrong.

Not an insane notion, on the face of it. Except for one thing.

I didn't have his phone number.

Oh, I had the number for *Random Access*, but calling the BBS meant a trip upstairs, firing up the computer, dialing, logging on, paging and . . .

"The hell with it," I told the kitchen, steam winning over dismay. I clicked the tiny purse shut and headed for the ell, high heels snapping against the linoleum.

I had my hand on the door when the phone rang.

The answering machine picked up on the fourth ring and I turned away from the door, listening to my recorded voice advising the caller to wait for the beep.

Bee-ep.

"Jennifer, it's Fox." He paused, long enough for me to cross the room to Communications Central and pick up the receiver.

"Hi," I said flatly.

"Good. I was afraid you'd left." Relief sounded clearly. "Can you wait another few minutes and we'll be fashionably late for the masquerade?"

Steam and dismay had vanished like fog under sunlight. "Sure," I said, then, grabbing a pen out of the holder and clicking the point out, commanded, "Give me your phone number."

"Don't you have it? Stupid of me." He recited seven quick digits and I wrote them down on the resident notepad with a scrawled "Fox" beside them.

"It wouldn't have done you any good this evening, I'm afraid. One of my clients called, wanting me to troubleshoot over the phone, which is what's kept me." He sighed. "I could *not* get him off the phone."

I laughed. "But did you fix the problem?"

"That's the worst of it–I'm going to have to fly down to Virginia and actually look at the problem. Listen, I'll be over in about ten minutes, all right?"

"All right. Watch out for deer."

"I'll be careful," he promised. "See you soon."

"Bye."

I cradled the receiver, flipped open my personal phone book and transcribed Fox's number under F, then closed the book, stowed the pen and opened the tiny satin bag to put my keys away.

*

The Mill is located on River Street, about a mile out of the center of town. A grist mill had once stood upon the site now graced by Wimsy's luxury restaurant and hotel; the restaurant's back wall had been built from stones belonging to the original mill, which had been abandoned ninety years ago and allowed to decay. Grant McElroy of Boston, Mass. bought the land from the town two years ago–just prior to my hitting town–boasting that he was going to build the town a five-star eating and sleeping showplace. Nobody was more surprised than the councilors who'd signed off on the deal when he actually made good on his boast. I hadn't been in the place since the pre-opening tour-and-tea-party for Important Folks and the press.

Fox pulled the emerald green four-by-four into the only vacant parking spot in three counties and killed the engine.

"We arrive at the masquerade," he informed me, voice grave as always.

"So we do," I allowed, austerely. "Let us then alight and masque."

"I like that," he said. "Whom shall we be?"

I glanced over at his silhouette. "It's not a real masquerade," I told him. "You knew that."

"An unreal masquerade," he murmured. "Even better." He opened his door.

By the time I'd unhooked the seatbelt, he was opening my door, holding up a hand to help me down, which courtesy I greatly appreciated. There had been a time when I'd been accustomed to navigating in high heels, but that was several years in the past. You do forget these things. I bet there are even people who've forgotten how to swim.

Fox shut the door, offered me his arm and we sauntered down the parking lot in the cold, the rosette glare from the Mill's lights shutting out the stars, and went in through the wide glass doors.

Inside, we followed discreetly posted signs across the lobby and down a short hallway, turning right into a secondary lobby fronted by double wooden doors. To the left of the door was a coat check.

I dropped Fox's arm and headed that way, gratefully tugging down on the parka's zipper.

"I think you ought to keep it with you," Fox murmured from beside me. "It makes something of a statement."

"Yes, but which statement?" I handed the parka across to the counter to the rosy-cheeked attendant and watched Fox deftly rid himself of his overcoat. Revealed at last, the tux was in the classic mode–black, white shirt, black-as-demanded tie. Perfection, in short, and worn with a definite air. I sighed in outright envy and he turned to look at me, one eyebrow up.

"Fox, you're beautiful. Really."

His mouth curved in his faint smile. "I return the compliment."

I smiled, ridiculously pleased.

"Excuse me." That was the coat-check girl, round-eyed and rosy-cheeked, her hair that particular shade of pale red that Harry Pelletier assures me is *blonde.* We both turned to look at her.

"Excuse me," she said again, her cheeks a little rosier than they had been a moment ago. "I couldn't help but overhear–are you Fox? I mean, Fox-who-runs-the-computer-board?"

"I'm afraid so."

"Oh." Her round blue eyes got rounder and she looked at me. "And you? I don't mean to be rude, but I'm Lisa–Lisa Gagnon and . . ."

"Hi, Lisa," I smiled and put out my hand. "I'm Jen Pierce."

"Oh, how *neat*," she squealed, grabbing my hand and holding on tight. "This is *so* neat, to really meet people that I've only–well, we've met, but–you know what I mean?" she finished, hopefully.

"I know what you mean," I assured her, rescuing my hand and smiling again.

She was smiling too. "My, the two of you are elegant. I had no idea."

"We're not always elegant," Fox said seriously. "We happen to be on our way to a masquerade."

"Oh, at Christmas?" she said doubtfully, then rallied. "But isn't that cunning! Who are you supposed to–no, I know! Prince Charles and Princess Di! Am I right?"

Both of Fox's eyebrows went up. He glanced at me.

"Gomez and Morticia Addams?" he asked ruminatively. I gave him the best glare I could muster under the circumstances and turned back to Lisa.

"Actually, no one you know," I said brightly. "It's a little in-joke. We're—uhh—we're dressed as Fox's parents."

"Oh, excellent," I heard Fox murmur. "I like that one, Jennifer. Very much." And before I could do any more glaring, he stepped forward, swept an as-God-is-my-witness *bow* and once again offered me his arm.

"Colonel and Mrs. Foxwell!" he announced to Lisa's round-eye amaze, and flicked an evil glance into my face. "Jennifer, you are in for a rare evening. Shall we?"

It would seem that I had no choice. I flung a smile at Lisa and took up the gauntlet.

*

Predictably, the first person we encountered was Milt Vane, looking disreputable as only Milt can in a peacock blue tux and matching ruffle. He slammed to a halt, which sent the amber liquid sloshing in his glass, mouth and eyes forming three Os of astonishment.

It's Milt's curse that he can never stay silent long.

"Well," he announced, in his patented, carry-to-the-ends-of-the-universe drawl. "If it isn't the Snow Queen!"

I tensed. For my ears only, Fox murmured, "Friend of yours?"

"Not so you'd notice," I muttered back.

"Then there's no need to speak to him," Fox decided and guided me to Milt's left, pointedly not seeing same, and over to an empty table against the far wall.

There, he seated me—pulled out the chair and held it patiently while I sat, then helped me establish the most comfortable chair-to-table ratio before sitting beside me.

"Now," he said calmly, "if you are going to be Adele Foxwell, Jennifer, you must bear in mind that all these delightful people *want* to do things for you. It is your duty and your burden to allow them to serve, and thus to be happy. All right?"

I turned to stare at him. "Just what are you doing?"

He lifted an eyebrow. "A little experiment in social engineering, which should prove interesting. My mother is British, you see, and keeps my father to certain standards of respect and deference–which, by the way, he seems genuinely happy to maintain." A shadow flitted across his face, gone in a heartbeat. "They've been married forty years."

"Now," he said after a moment. "What I think will happen is that, as people observe our behavior–upscale and genteel as it must be–they will–with the possible exception of the execrable person we just passed–adjust their behavior accordingly. What do you think?"

"I think you're demented," I told him truthfully.

"Let me fetch you a glass of wine," Fox said, and left me.

I watched him cross the room, and saw more than one pair of feminine eyes follow. I didn't blame any of them–Kathy Foxwell's notion of what suited her man had been smack on the money.

Fox reappeared, carrying two glasses of white wine. He placed mine before me like it was the Grail and I the Lady of the Lake, then reseated himself at my side.

"To adventures," he said, raising his glass, and I couldn't help but laugh and raise mine, too.

"To adventures. Which are cold, uncomfortable and time-consuming."

We tapped glasses and sipped.

I'd barely replaced the Grail when a familiar voice said, "This looks like a good place to park."

Fox glanced up, inclined his bright head.

"Mr. Jacques."

Bill Jacques was wearing a black tie, as required. He was also wearing a charcoal gray business suit and a white dress shirt. His blunt face registered neither surprise nor chagrin at his greeting; rather he inclined his head, and did a very creditable job of reproducing Fox's intonation: "Mr. Foxwell." Another inclination: "Ms. Pierce."

"Mr. Jacques," I murmured.

Bill placed a light hand on his companion's arm. "Peggy, I think you know my friend Mr. Foxwell."

Gold lame was apparently Peggy Neuman's material of choice. This evening it was in the shape of a scooped neck mini-dress with a full flirty skirt that set off those long, long legs. She grinned. "Hi, Foxy."

He accepted her salutation with yet another bow of the head. "Ms. Neuman."

"And this," Bill said, bringing her attention to me. "Is Jennifer Pierce. Jennifer, this is my friend Peggy Neuman."

"Hi," she said, grin getting wider, and stuck out her hand.

I met it and returned the grin. "I've seen your act."

She laughed. "And I've read your articles. We're even. Bill, would you fetch me a glass of the usual?"

"Sure." He turned, checked and turned back to Fox. "Are these seats taken, sir?"

"Not unless you and the lady will honor us."

"Wow," said Peggy. She pulled out a chair and sank onto the edge, crossing her legs in one smooth motion. "I'll hold the fort," she told Bill. He nodded and went away.

"So, Foxy, what is this?" she asked, crossing her arms on the table and leaning forward. "Looking very sharp, by the way."

"Thank you." He sipped his wine. "It's a masquerade."

"It's Christmas time, Foxy. This is called an office party, though I don't get it myself. Thought the *Voice* would throw more like a pizza-and-beer office party."

"Is there a rule against masquerades at Christmas?" Fox asked seriously.

"Hey, nobody ever sent me the rule book," she said

and reached over to pat his hand. "Masquerade away, if it makes you happy."

"Here we go." Bill Jacques set a tumbler filled with dark brown carbonation, sporting a cherry and a yellow umbrella before Peggy and pulled out the chair beside her. Deliberately, he poured beer from the bottle into his glass, then looked over at Fox.

"Want to tell me about it?"

"It's an experiment in social engineering," Fox said. "I mentioned to the coat-check clerk that we were going to a masquerade party and Jennifer came up with the notion that we attend as my parents."

Peggy gave a shout of laughter, then shook her head. "You," she said, raising her glass, "are not a nice man."

Fox lifted his eyebrows. "Oh?" he said interestedly.

She sighed and looked across to me. "It's the hair," she explained earnestly. "I honestly think that the world would be a saner, safer place if all redheads had their hair therapeutically dyed brown."

"I don't want brown hair," Fox said.

"It's for your own good," Bill Jacques told him, pouring more beer. He glanced up. "And for the safety of your loved ones."

"A compelling argument, I agree."

"I was sure you would," Bill said placidly and sipped his beer.

12

The River Room, the largest of the Mill's banquet rooms, wasn't large, though it was more than roomy enough to accommodate the bar, the buffet, and seating sufficient to the *Voice*'s twenty-seven employees, their dates and/or significant others. Occasionally, a bell or an organ note from the chirpy piped-in Christmas music would make itself heard around the edge of the general babble.

Sartorially speaking, my colleagues had achieved noteworthiness. Red and green were the chosen colors for dresses that were long and short, but uniformly low-cut, and there were of course an abundance of blue and pink tuxes, of the sort popular for prom wear. Bobby Leconte, nightside paste-up, took the prize for best overall presentation, male, with his full vanilla tails, pale lilac shirt and cummerbund, white vest a-glitter with beaded crystal flowers.

"And not a baby grand in sight," Bill Jacques commented as our table unanimously awarded the impromptu–and wholly imaginary–prize. "If we had known you were going to be here, Mr. Liberace . . ."

"No, he's dressed down, see?" Peggy protested, pointing with the yellow paper umbrella that had lately adorned her "usual."

"Incognito?" Bill frowned at Bobby's dazzling back. "You could be right."

"Better incognito than dead," I said.

"We have a Liberace sighting," Fox intoned. "Shall I phone *The Inquirer* or does that honor belong to Mr. Jacques?"

"I think it has to be Bill, don't you?" I said, and grinned as he turned to stare at me. "Your stature as an editor," I explained, "must of course lend credence."

"Of course," Bill said politely. "David, you're a bad influence on my reporter."

"Oh, dear," Fox murmured, opening his eyes wide. "A *very* bad influence or only moderate?"

"The jury's still out," Bill said. "But I'd prepare myself for the worst."

"Anything worth doing is worth doing well," Fox told him gravely.

"A bird in hand is worth two in the bush," Bill agreed with equal gravity.

"Speaking of which," I put in, more to put a halt to Dueling Proverbs than because I wanted to know, "where are The Twins?"

"They seduced all of you away from the newspaper this evening so they could blow up the building and collect the insurance money," Fox suggested.

"The Twins would want all of us *in* the building if they were going to blow it up," I told him. He lifted an eyebrow.

"Unfortunate, but accurate," Bill said and glanced over to Peggy. "Would you care to go in to supper, Ms. Neuman?"

She grinned. "After I go in to the ladies." She stood. Fox stood. Bill stood. In the general spirit of cooperation, I stood, taking a firm grip on my tiny bag.

Peggy grinned at me and together we left the table.

*

In the mirrored anteroom of the Ladies Lounge, I fluttered some powder on my nose, twisted the brush closed and dropped it into my bag. The click of high heels on tile brought my eyes up.

Peggy Neuman strode into the anteroom on her mile-long legs and grinned at me in the mirror.

"That is a *hot* dress," she said, husky voice admiring. "Boston?"

I shook my head. "Cinderella Shoppe."

"Really?" She came up next to me in the mirror. "Old Miss Dostie–God, she must be a hundred by now!–had that dress in her shop?"

"Actually, no. Miss Dostie sold the store and moved to Florida. The new owner's a Colby grad–Mike Parmentier."

"Mike made a few changes, did he?"

"She," I corrected as Peggy ran her fingers into her blond mane. "The formal is Eustacie. Mike to her friends."

"Well, sure. Would you be Eustacie one minute longer than you had to?" She gave her hair a vigorous shake and looked at me in the mirror. "Known Foxy long?"

The frontal attack. I shrugged, aware of the dress moving with me. "A couple months," I said. "Known Bill long?" No rules against returning the favor.

Peggy laughed and shook her hair once more.

"Bill and I dated in high school. I always figured he'd graduate, go away to college and move on to do great things. He was the kind of guy you thought would do great things–smart, serious, steady." She turned to face me, hands on gold lame hips. "Could've knocked me over with a feather when he came walking into the Chez to see my show. Last person I expected to see again in this lifetime was Billy Jacques."

I looked at her. "Are you sorry?"

She shook her head, mane swirling, and smiled along one side of her mouth. "I'm not sorry," she said. "Comes to me that maybe I didn't value steady quite enough, when I was fifteen."

"That does tend to come later," I agreed, thinking of my own early and failed marriage.

"And now it's later, but maybe not too late," Peggy said, and took my arm. "We'd better be getting back to the gentlemen."

"Before they pine away, you mean?"

She gave me another of her wide grins. "That's the idea."

Arm-in-arm, we navigated the floor, which was

cluttered here and there with knots and tangles of people: Pink tuxedos and green-and-red dresses. I waved across the room at a huddle composed of Sue Danforth and Nanci Sennett and got a pair of waves and a couple smiles in return.

We were just detouring around the last knot between us and our table when a hand shot forth and closed on my arm.

"Jen!" cried Carly, who was attached to the hand. She stepped quickly to my side.

"Hi, Carly," I said, standing as patiently as I could while her fingers grooved the flesh beneath the satin sleeve. I used my chin to point at Peggy, standing quietly at my side. "This is Peggy Neuman. Peggy, this is Carly Saunders."

Carly was dressed in a proliferation of iridescent tissue gauze, which should have made her look like a box of metallic Kleenex, or possibly a mutated chrysanthemum, but actually made her look buxom, luxurious and abundant. She threw a vague smile in Peggy's direction.

"Hi."

"Pleased to meet you," Peggy answered, but Carly was back on me like a kitten on a feather. "Jennifer, where on *earth* did you get *him*?"

I blinked. "Him?"

"Your *date*," Carly said, with more urgency that I thought the question merited. "Who *is* he?"

"Oh." I slid a glance sideways, saw Bill and Fox gazing interestedly in our direction and looked back to Carly. "He's a friend of Bill's."

"What's his name?"

I was starting to get annoyed. "Carly, look–"

"His name's David," Peggy said from my side. "Why don't you come to the table and introduce yourself? I'm sure he'd be happy to meet you."

Carly blinked and glanced over her shoulder at a slope-shouldered young man in a green tuxedo who was watching her pointedly.

"Um—sure," Carly said, dropping my arm all at once and stepping back. The man in green took a half-step toward her. "We'll stop by later. Thanks, Jen."

"OK," I said and did not shake my head, though I wanted to. Peggy and I moved on.

"What was that all about?" Bill wanted to know, after he and Fox had risen and we were all four seated again.

I sighed, still irritated. "Oh, Carly wants to ravish Fox."

Fox's eyebrows rose.

"What's the matter, Foxy?" Peggy asked huskily. "You don't want to be ravished?"

There was a small pause. "I'm saving myself for someone who knows the difference between me and my shiny shoes," he answered.

"Very wise," Bill judged, pushing back from the table. "Ravished is as ravished does and I don't know about the rest of you people, but I ravish much better when I've been fed."

"Dinner!" Peggy came to her feet and slid her arm through Bill's. They moved away.

I glanced over at Fox.

"Hungry, Jennifer?" he asked quietly.

"I could eat," I allowed and bit my lip. "Carly's harmless."

"But irritating."

I sighed. "She's not that bad. My temper's another story, though."

"And *your* hair is naturally brown," he said and rose, holding my chair while I did likewise, then offering the support of his arm for the long trek downroom to the buffet.

*

We'd finished eating and had received a few visitors—Sue Danforth; Dan and Ginny Skat; Carly and her escort, introduced as "Evan," who spent the entire five minutes of small talk glaring at Fox; and Milt Vane, naturally enough, escorting his usual petite, pretty and numbingly silly date. Tonight's usual was raven haired, with eyes of that improbable shade of turquoise that can only be achieved by tinted contacts. She stood quietly under the arm Milt had draped across her shoulders and smiled at a point somewhere near the center of the table. I think her name was Tina.

"Where does he get them?" I asked Bill after Milt had finally gone away, steering Tina by the shoulders.

"Catalog out of Indiana somewhere, I believe." He glanced across the room and then swiftly back to Peggy. "I have sighted a Talbot in the crowd," he told her, "and discover an urgent desire to be elsewhere. What's your mood?"

"Elsewhere suits," she said and rose, smiling at me and then at Fox. "You two might want to slip away, too, from all Bill's told me about this pair."

"But only think how rude it would be in me, not to speak with my hosts," Fox protested.

Peggy laughed and slipped her arm through Bill's. "Some people take manners too far," she said.

"Some people are very brave." Bill inclined his head. "David. Jennifer. We'll be walking out, now. Thank you for a delightful evening."

"Frequent exercise is important to the maintenance of good health," Fox said by way of farewell and our tablemates strolled off, angling toward the door and the lobby beyond.

"Well." Fox looked over to me. "Jennifer, I wonder if I can ask you to do a favor for me."

I blinked at him. "What kind of favor?"

"A simple favor," he said promptly, smiling his slight smile. "Possibly even enjoyable. I wonder if you'd keep an eye on *Random Access* for me while I go down to Virginia and put out Mr. Wilkie's fire."

It actually was an enjoyable favor. I've been co-sysop on a couple boards in my day, though I never had enough tenacity to build and maintain my own. However, while enjoyable, the favor was *not* simple. It required, in fact, rather a leap of faith on the part of the sysop sitting beside me.

"I'll need access to the back door," I reminded him, which in plain language meant that *Random Access* would be totally vulnerable, laid wide open for me to hack, dismantle or destroy, as whim might take me.

"Nothing easier," Fox said calmly. "I'll key you in tomorrow. Also, if you have time tomorrow afternoon, you could stop by and take a look at the system."

"I'd like that," I said around a warm glow of pleasure. "I've got a delivery coming around two . . . Will three o'clock be OK for you?"

"Three it is," he said and seemed about to say something else, but John Talbot beat him to it.

"Well, well, Ms. Pierce. Having a nice time?"

I looked up. John was wearing the second of what was probably a total of three black tuxedos in the room and, in justice, he wore it well, though I was inclined to think Fox wore his with more flair. The woman on John's arm was again in red, the fabric this evening was velvet.

"I'm having a good time, Mr. Talbot. Thank you," I said with composure, then turned my brightest professional smile on his companion as I held out my hand. "Ms. Jefferson, how nice to see you again."

"Ms. Pierce." She smiled her cool smile and met my hand for a brief shake. I rested my liberated fingers on Fox's sleeve.

"This is Serena Jefferson and John Talbot," I told him; and to them, "David Foxwell."

John inclined his head, doing the gracious host. "Mr. Foxwell. I hope you're enjoying yourself?"

"Very much," Fox replied with his accustomed gravity.

"Foxwell . . ." Serena Jefferson was frowning slightly. Fox raised his eyebrows. She smiled and shook her head.

"I beg your pardon," she said, with an air of reciting a phrase, the meaning of which she had long forgotten. "You put me in mind of another Foxwell I had met—some years ago, now." She treated Fox to another frosty smile. "That man was on the President's staff, as I recall it. A military man."

"Air Force," Fox said and inclined his head. "My father."

"Indeed." I got the distinct feeling that she was impressed, though all she did was nod politely. "Are you also in the Air Force?"

"My father had hoped for pilot's training," Fox murmured. "Unfortunately, I require corrective lenses."

"I see." She seemed to suddenly become aware again of John's presence, and smiled impartially at both of us. "It was delightful seeing you again, Ms. Pierce. Mr. Foxwell, a pleasure."

"Good-night," I told her, giving her smile back to her. Fox murmured a secondary farewell, but John was already steering her toward the next table.

I sighed and glanced over, to find Fox watching me.

"Had enough fun for one night?" I asked, only half kidding.

"I believe so. Thank you for a most instructive evening."

"You asked for it, remember?" I rose and picked up my bag, then took Fox's arm for the promenade to the lobby.

*

The drive home was accomplished with a comfortable lack of conversation, Enya playing quietly on the CD player. Fox pulled up to the porch and left the truck idling while he came around to open my door and help me out. I took his arm—and blinked at him in the combined light from porch and headlights.

"Fox?"

He slipped his arm away, eyes shadowed by auburn lashes. "It's all right, Jennifer."

"All right?" I asked, concern making my tone sharper than I'd intended. "My God, you're shaking like a leaf! You must be frozen—" But it had been warm in the truck.

"I'm fine," he said and slid a not-quite-steady hand under my elbow, guiding me up the steps, across the porch, to my door.

"At least come in and let me give you some coffee," I said as he took his hand away and stepped back. He shook his head.

"I'm fine," he repeated, mouth tightening in what he may have thought was a smile. "I had a good time this evening."

"I had a good time, too," I told him truthfully, then blurted, "Come in and get warm."

The smile this time was nearer his norm. He shook his head and went back a step. "It's just ten minutes to home," he said, and went back another step. "Good-night, Jennifer. Lock the door."

I hesitated another heartbeat, but really, what could I do, hit him on the head and drag him inside?

"Good-night," I said finally, clicking open the bag and fishing out my keys. "I'll see you around three tomorrow."

"That's right," he said and watched me use the key to let myself in. He was still watching when I closed the door behind me and shot the deadbolt home.

13

The Currier estate sits well outside of town, two miles beyond the Mill along the River Road, then another mile up the Winding Road. The main house is built of native rock, hauled up, as I imagine it, boulder by boulder from the surrounding fields.

Along the span of five or six generations, the Curriers went from farmers and salt-of-the-earth to lawyers and pillars-of-the-community. The last Currier to live in the now-abandoned big house had been a judge.

With the judge's death, the house and surrounding fields, now leased to local farmers, fell to a gaggle of grandchildren and great-grands, all of whom had jobs, families and lives of their own and none of whom could conceive of taking on the care and feeding of the enormous old white elephant at the top of Winding Hill.

Nor could they, after rabid interfamily politics had taken the issue to several votes, produce from among their numbers a majority committed to sell.

And so the big house was boarded up, after being relieved of its more valuable contents by those grands and greats with a taste for the antique. A trust was set up out of the judge's cash assets, which, with the addition of the field leases and the income from the modernized carriage house, had so far produced enough to cover the property taxes on the place.

Fox lives in the carriage house.

The iron gates that guard the entrance to the grand drive at the pinnacle of Winding Hill are of course chained tight. Access to the carriage house is a quarter-mile before the gates: an insignificant-looking dirt drive angling off into a tangle of scrub pine and cedar.

Constructed in the year of my birth, the carriage house had never been precisely that. It was originally built to accommodate a maiden aunt with leanings toward Art, and had since her death housed a series of cousins, Worthy Causes, and now, in the eighth year of the reign of the grands and great-grands, *boarders*.

The Camaro minced down the stone-hard drive, taking the unfamiliar curves with cautious arrogance. It would not do to hit a deer, or a cat, or any other wandering small life that might be abroad in this frigid, fading afternoon.

It was precisely three o'clock by the dashboard clock when the driveway surrendered me to a broad, pink-bricked yard. I slid the Camaro in next to Fox's green four-by-four, killed the engine and took a moment to stare.

Consider the Gingerbread House in the Deep Wood. Color it Tudor, with half-timbered, whitewashed walls and wide mullioned windows giving back the fading light like ten thousand tiny prisms. The deeply pitched roof is tin, painted dark brown, overhanging the front windows and door in the classic necessity of Maine architecture—a snow-break.

I popped the driver's side door and stepped out onto the rough pink brick.

The front door was recessed, the arch outlined in stone; the door itself of dark, shiny wood, broken by a single octagonal window. Centered below it hung a knocker like an iron fist.

I lifted the fist and let it fall against the hammer-plate.

The wind rustled the arborvitae planted along the front of the house, to my right.

From inside, I heard the snap of a lock coming back, then the door swung wide and away and Fox was smiling his faint smile, stepping back to let me in.

"Good afternoon, Jennifer."

"Hi."

The foyer was laid with flagstone, perfect depository for winter's snowy boots. There was a bench along the right wall, pegs along the left. Fox's hooded blue coat occupied the peg farthest from the door. I slipped the purple parka off and hung it on the next.

"Did you have any trouble finding me?" Fox asked.

I turned and smiled. "Your directions were great. Didn't even have to go to the top of the hill to turn around and try again."

"Success," he agreed.

The flannel shirt today was black-and-white check, two buttons open at the throat; the jeans were a hundred launderings past indigo. Tennis shoes, not new. Battered leather belt. And over it all, like a good wool sweater, Fox's accustomed grave self-possession.

I felt my smile widen.

He lifted an eyebrow. "Yes?"

I almost told him that I'd been worried about him, which would have been the truth, but hardly consistent with my general policy of keeping people at an emotional arm's length. So I looked around the paneled foyer, noticing the electric candles in their crystal globes above the bench, then back to Fox.

"Nice house."

"Wait until you see the rest of it," he said, coming forward to slip a hand under my elbow. He turned me toward the end of the foyer. "Vintage Gertrude Stein."

I laughed and he flicked a cobalt glance into my face. "You don't believe me?"

"The trouble is, I *do* believe you," I said and let myself be navigated through an arch and into the main room.

The bronze flocked wallpaper testified to the room's former function. This had once been the Salon, where the artsy aunt gathered with her artsy friends to read aloud, to critique works in progress and those long published, to indulge in the Creative Pose and to incidentally drink the aunt's refreshment and consume her comestibles. That had been some time ago, when the oriental carpet had been a plush scarlet oasis centered in an acre of unscarred hardwood floor.

Some glory remained. The aunt would certainly have approved the grouping before the stone fireplace: the bronze damask covering the sofas was perhaps in need of cleaning, the deep green velvet of the armchairs was maybe, just a bit, faded. The green and bronze curtains along the floor-to-ceiling window were authentically shabby; the wooden interior shutters as scarred and in need of revarnishing as the floor they matched.

To one side of the conversation group, someone had placed a very modern, very expensive sound system, speakers hung precisely so that the central damask sofa would receive the best benefit of their stereo. An anachronism, but only a small one: Surely the aunt would have welcomed music and musicians into the Salon.

I took one step forward.

The entrance arch was near the top of the room; to my right was a narrow alcove, which must have once housed the refreshment table. Now, it held a computer desk, complete with a wide and rather scruffy desktop CPU. Atop this venerable unit reposed a spanking new, or close enough, twenty-one-inch monitor, which was currently displaying a starfield, as seen from the observation deck of the Starship Enterprise, underway at Warp One. A laser printer sat to the right, a college student's cheap swing-arm metal lamp, considerably dented and presently dark, was facing the wall. To the left, a mahogany table, with ornately carved legs, that must have been original with the room supported approximately fifty pounds of papers and documentation.

To my left, along the wall shared with the foyer, a long library table, also mahogany, held a desktop scanner, a midget photocopier, a switchbox bristling with phone lines, a laptop computer and a Kilimanjaro of CD jewel-cases and disk file boxes.

A corner shelf was built into the angle of inner and front walls: it had once doubtless held various breakables and bric-a-brac such as a maiden lady with pretensions to art might choose to display.

On it now reposed a computer, screen, keyboard and a small fleet of outriggers—backpack CD players, portable hard drives, more jewel-cases and disk-boxes, a pad of paper, several pens, a tangle of cable like nestling king snakes.

"*Random Access,*" Fox murmured from behind me. "Would you like a closer look?"

*

It was six-fifteen by the time *Random Access* had been thoroughly explored. We'd adjourned to the kitchen and I was sitting at the table, watching Fox do efficient things with the coffee maker.

"Milk and no sugar," he didn't ask over his shoulder.

"Right," I agreed and he carried two stoneware mugs over. I took one and he retained custody of the other as he sat in the chair across from me.

"Feel comfortable with it?"

I nodded and took a cautious sip from my mug. "I think I'll be OK for anything short of a hot-boot."

"Oh." Fox put his mug down and stood up. "I knew there was something else," he said apologetically, slipping a hand into his pocket. In a moment, he laid a bright silver key on the table before me and sat down again.

I blinked.

"That's a copy of the front door key," he explained, carefully, I thought. "In case the board needs a hot-boot." He sipped his coffee. "Which it does sometimes, though not often. However, Murphy's Law clearly states that if the sysop goes out of town without leaving a key to the front door with some knowledgeable person the board will go down two seconds after the sysop has driven out of the dooryard."

"Too true." I sipped coffee and did not look at the shiny-bright key on the table before me. "When are you leaving?"

"Tomorrow morning. With any luck at all, I'll resolve Mr. Wylie's little difficulty and be back home Monday evening." He lifted an eyebrow. "I'll call you. All right?"

"Sure." I drank coffee, letting matters turn themselves over in my mind, in case one came up a question.

"The Internet feed takes care of itself?" I asked, feeling my mouth quirk. "Speaking of Murphy's Law."

"Right you are." He had a sip, considering. "The feed's been taking care of itself beautifully," he said at last. "Which of course means that it's due for a major failure. However, since we have no idea which attack the Hun will favor . . ."

"Light candles, chant and think good thoughts."

"That seems the best course," Fox agreed solemnly. I grinned and finished my coffee.

"Well, I'd better get out of here and let you pack." I stood. My right hand moved in a swoop, capturing the shiny key: the aluminum felt cool against my palm.

Fox rose and walked me to the foyer, took the purple parka from its peg and held it ready for me to slip on.

"Thanks." The zipper went up like it was supposed to for a change. I pulled car keys from my pocket.

"Thank you," he returned, unlocking and opening the front door. The porch light came on as I stepped outside, a cone of yellow, holding back the dark.

"Drive carefully," Fox said as I went down the pink walk. "I'll call you when I get home."

14

Sunday evenings at the *Voice* have an air of picnic about them. Carly often brings in a homebaked goody; Dan Skat sometimes contributes cheese and crackers. My offerings are usually apple-based, either on the hoof or in the shape of cider, as Morris DuChamp's notion of how much of either one woman and a cat can put away tends toward the heroic. Sometimes Bill Jacques will order in a bucket of chicken and we'll all break for dinner when it arrives, sitting four around the glass-topped conference table, forking cole slaw out of the same quart container and deciding world policy between mouthfuls of spicy-fried drumsticks.

Tonight's treat was a collaboration. Earlier in the week, I'd given Carly a couple dozen Northern Spy. This evening, some of them had come back to the newsroom in the form of apple crunch cake.

Around five-thirty, having typed all the briefs in my stack and taken two obits, I pushed back from my computer, stretched, picked up my mug and headed toward Dayside, where the coffeepot lives.

I poured myself a generous mugful, dusted in some non-dairy coffee whitener, paid tribute to the apple crunch, of which about half remained, and glanced up at the sound of approaching footsteps.

"Ah, Mr. Jacques," I said, as he hove 'round the corner. "Come to admire culinary art?"

"From a distance," he said, putting his mug next to mine. He hefted the coffeepot and slugged some thick brown juice into his mug. I picked up my mug and turned away.

"Jen."

I turned back, surprised into a gawp, and blinked into

his blunt face. "What's wrong?" I blurted.

His mouth twisted– wry humor–and he shook his head.

"Nothing's wrong–and it's nothing that's any of my business, either." He picked up the jar of non-dairy whitener and shook a minor blizzard into the steam above his cup. "But, if you're dating David Foxwell . . ."

I set my mug down carefully. "I'm not *dating* him–" I began. Bill shook his head and turned to look at me, face earnest.

"David's OK," he said, "it's nothing like that. It's just that . . ." He took a breath, looking uncomfortable, and Bill never looks uncomfortable. "That his wife . . ."

"His wife died a couple years ago," I said, crisply, since he was having so much trouble spitting it out. "I know."

He nodded, but didn't look particularly relieved. "Good. But what you might not know is that–I get the sense that he's not– exactly–over it–yet."

I felt my mouth tighten. "And how–exactly–does somebody get–over– something like that?" I asked, and heard the snap of sarcasm in my voice.

If Bill heard it, he gave no sign, but looked at me again with that earnest and entirely serious expression. "People do," he said, voice matching his face. "You wouldn't think so, but if the first strike doesn't kill you, it's likely you'll make it back. It takes some people longer than others, but sooner or later, they start reaching out. Start remembering the why behind the forms they've been going through on automatic. Start . . . coming to life again." He picked up his mug and took a swallow. If the coffee burned his mouth, he didn't flinch.

"David's my friend," he said, quietly. "And I'd like to think that you are, too. I don't want to see either of you hurt."

I blinked. Of course I knew Bill and Fox were friends. I liked Bill myself, editor or not. But the idea that Bill considered me as friend–had never actually occurred to me. I don't have many friends. Never have. I'm not very good at people.

Fox though . . . Memory helpfully provided a collage: Fox and Marian, heads bent together as they studied a computer's innards; Fox, shopping alone late at night; Fox entirely oblivious to Janice Younger's advances. Fox, shaking like a malaria victim as he helped me to my door. Fox, who had come to Maine to avenge his wife's murder—and set up a computer bulletin board, giving him access to people twenty-four hours a day—as much or as little as he wanted. All he had to do was hit "chat".

BBS users tend to forget, I thought suddenly, that the bulletin board has value for the sysop, too.

I took a breath and looked up to Bill, and said the only thing I could think of.

"Thanks."

"Any time," he said, and swallowed some more coffee.

*

Back at my desk, I went through the last week's papers, tearing out the pages containing my stories. It was mindless work, a typical chore for Sunday, when things were often dull and quiet. Even the scanner was quiet tonight. Dan Skat stopped to fiddle with it on his way to the coffeepot, but all he got was static, way at the top of the gain. He grunted and turned it down again.

I put the papers I didn't want on top of my computer so I'd remember to take them back to the recycling bin later, then sorted my tearsheets by subject and filed them in the left-hand desk drawer.

The scanner squawked as I closed the drawer, then Ken Aube's voice, unmistakable over a line suddenly static-free and clean.

"Ten-forty-four at the Mill," he said and I spun in my chair, notebook leaping to my hand. Ten-forty-four is cop-code for suspicious death.

"On it," the dispatcher said, and I yelled "Dan!" and

ran for my coat.

*

We beat the medical examiner to the scene, which wasn't surprising, and also the State Police, which was. Dan Skat was out of the passenger's seat before I'd thrown the Camaro into park, a square-chested silhouette charging across the glare of the headlights. I killed the engine, retracted my seatbelt and went after him, though not so headlong as he: I'm a graceless runner and find a brisk walk gets me from A to B just as quickly and a lot more neatly.

Moving at the top of my pace, I wove through the confusion on the sidewalk—restaurant patrons, I guessed, who were swamping Wimsy Patrolman Vince Kellor with questions. I slipped past and into the lobby, where I found Patrolman Albert Giguere standing in front of the elevators. Dan was nowhere in sight.

"Ms. Pierce," Albert said in his slow, careful voice. "You know I can't let you go up there."

"Sure," I said, smiling. "Can you tell me what's going on? I heard the ten-forty-four over the scanner."

"Well, then, you know as much as I can tell you," Albert said. "Guest heard what sounded like a gunshot, phoned the desk. Mr. McElroy went on up, found the body."

I nodded. "Know who it is?"

Albert shrugged. "Got a tentative ID, based on the maids' schedules."

I blinked, switching gears. "One of the staff was shot?" I repeated, while my brain helpfully provided scenarios. Back when I'd first come on at the *Voice*, we'd had a particularly terrible murder come down. A much-decorated Viet Nam vet, sadly prone to flashbacks, shot his wife to death while she was doing the gardening, thinking she was Charlie. Last I heard, he was still in the Bangor Mental Health Insitute.

"Surprised a guest?" I asked Albert, but he shook his

head.

"Anything I tell you's going to be pure speculation. You're just going to have to wait to find out, just like me."

"Can't blame me for trying," I quipped, though he might at that. I get the impression that Albert thinks his life would be a lot easier without newspapers–or reporters–in it.

He gave me a tight-lipped smile and seemed about to say something, but the commotion at the door claimed his attention. I saw the State Trooper uniforms out of the corner of my eye, looked around, spied the sign for the restrooms and headed in that direction. I didn't look back to see if Albert had paid attention to my departure. No reason for him to be bothered by a girl going to the ladies, especially when she was headed directly away from the elevators.

*

There was a policeman on the service stairs, naturally enough, but there wasn't anyone at all–in uniform or out–at the door to the staff room, off the kitchen corridor. I eased the door open carefully, my story ready, but I needn't have worried: the staff room was empty.

I saw what I wanted right away–a corkboard with the Workman's Compensation poster and other official state papers tacked to it. In amidst it all was a schedule sheet, eerily similar to the sheet at the *Voice*. I ran my finger down the column for Sunday night, to the single name, hand-printed in neat letters.

Lisa Gagnon, night maid.

"Oh, no," I breathed, and it sounded like a prayer in my own ears.

*

Dan Skat was already belted into the passenger's seat of my car when I slid into the driver's side.

"Where'd you get to?" I asked him, not really caring.

My mind was still busy with denial. Maybe Lisa had called in sick. Maybe she'd switched shifts. Maybe . . .

"I went up to get a picture," Dan said, and there was something . . . over-calm . . . in his voice that grabbed my attention. I turned in the seat, but all I could see was his profile as he stared straight ahead.

"So," I said, after a minute had passed and he hadn't said anything else. "Did you get a picture?"

He took a deep breath; I saw his shoulders rise with it, then fall.

"The *Voice* doesn't want the picture I got," he said, softly, and raised his hand to rub at his face. "God, no, it doesn't."

I bit my lip. "Dan, are you saying you got past the cop on the stairs and the cop on the room and actually got a picture of the– the–"

"Body," he finished. "Yeah. There wasn't anybody on the door. I heard Ken down the hall, asking somebody about cigarettes . . ."

"Cigarettes?" I repeated. At a time like this, with Lisa lying . . .

"It's what he said–cigarettes," Dan insisted. "Where's my damn' cigarettes–something like that. I was keeping an ear out, in case he should head back my way, but mostly I just wanted to grab the shot . . ." He made a small, puffing sound– maybe it was a laugh.

"So," I said again. "What–was it like?"

"Bad," he said simply. "Blood–on the walls, on the floor–just everywhere. Her head–she must've put the barrel in her mouth and pulled the trigger. Ate the gun, like cops say . . ." He shook his head. "It was still in her hand."

I swallowed, then shifted 'round in the seat, reaching up to pull the seatbelt across.

"Let's get back to the *Voice*," I said. "I've got some phone calls to make."

15

It was two a.m. when I pulled up to the full-service pump at the 24-hour Irving in Skowhegan, cut the motor, lowered the window and told the red-cheeked attendant to fill it up, premium.

He did. I handed him my card, signed the chit without looking at the total, sealed the window and pulled back onto 201, heading north.

Maine Route 201 runs from Quebec clear to the nether end of the state, though it joins up with U.S. 95 and a couple other routes down around Brunswick and loses its individuality. From Skowhegan south, it is a two-lane, pretty-well-kept, nicely behaved road, strongly reminiscent of U.S. Route 40 on the Baltimore-to-Jersey run.

Above Skowhegan, the road begins to assert itself, though it retains a thin veneer of politeness. At Moscow, twenty-five miles north of Skowhegan, fifty miles south of the Canadian border, 201 dispenses with manners altogether.

In short, it is not a route to be undertaken in the arctic deep night of a Maine December, with snow falling lightly out of a starless sky, without the direst provocation.

But I wasn't thinking of the season or the time as I pulled out of the Irving, heading north on the straight-route to Canada, and I certainly wasn't thinking about the switchback to be climbed on the far side of Moscow or the squirrely lane-and-a-half the straight-route became inside of Caratunk.

"You OK?" Bill Jacques asked, staring at me over the top of his glasses.

"I'm OK."

He stared a second or two longer, frowning, then went back to the screen. I stood there, staring at nothing in particular, or possibly at

Carly's workstation, dark and slightly seedy in her absence.

It was 12:30 a.m. Bill Jacques and I were the last in the newsroom. Chance Maurand was in like state, across the hall in paste-up; sipping a Coke, if I knew Chance, and waiting for The Story to come across so he could fill the hole on his final page, get Bill's OK and call it a night.

The Story.

The death-story, of course, for which the paper had been held, the presses, so to speak, halted. Page One, naturally. Above the fold, absolutely. Not a screamer head, because the Voice *wasn't like that. But a solid, no-nonsense fifty-incher, across four center columns—"Local Woman Shot to Death"—and then the subhead, half as high, half as dark, twice as long—"Mill Employee Killed Self, Police Theorize."*

"It's clean," Bill said and I shook myself out of my stare, nodded and wordlessly turned toward my desk.

"See you tomorrow," he said behind me.

"See you tomorrow," I replied. It didn't seem worth mentioning that tomorrow was already with us.

I passed the Agway on 201, the Camaro gathering speed as we headed for the Madison town line. The snow lay thicker on the fields up here, a fact I noted, then forgot, as my mind cycled back, worrying memory, rehashing disbelief . . .

The perky, credulous girl in the coat check booth, round eyes going even rounder as she giggled and gripped my hand. John Therriault's voice, cool in my ear, giving me ID—confirmed by Grant McElroy and the driver's license in the back pocket of the vicitm's jeans—approximate time of death, and method. A single gunshot wound to the head.

The Camaro and I topped Robbins Hill and headed down the long side toward Solon.

"Where'd she get the gun?" I asked John. He hesitated.

"We're guessing it was in the luggage. That's a guess, Jen. Not for publication."

"Luggage?" I repeated.

"Room was occupied; the guest was out."

I wrote on my pad, feeling an ache in my shoulder from holding the phone against my ear for so long. "So you'll be wanting to talk to the person who rented the room?"

"We'll talk to him," John said, flatly. "That's all I've got."

I slowed down as I passed the tiny Solon library, listening to John with memory's sharp ears.

Shot herself.

I braked, hard. Twisted the wheel right and pulled into the Solon Hotel's parking lot. The Hotel was dark, the Camaro the only car in the lot. I leaned back in the seat and listened to it again.

Shot herself.

Lisa *hated* guns. I swallowed, remembering all those tirades on *Random Access—*"I think the government should take all the guns away and melt them down to make cars out of." Right. And she'd made her husband get rid of his rifles before they got married, wasn't that it? Hunting was cruel. *Guns* were cruel; proximity to a firearm of any description made her feel physically ill.

What life event could be so traumatic, so mind-altering, to make a gun-phobe shoot herself?

I bit my lip, remembering her last message on *Random Access*: Her husband coming home, the certainty that it was going to work this time, the plans for a baby—where was the suicide there?

Memory provided a snapshot from Friday evening: Lisa, wide-eyed in the coat room, the hot lights lending fire to her pale red hair, blue eyes round and credulous in a rosy-cheeked, lightly freckled face.

Where was the suicide there?

What calamity had occurred between Friday and Sunday, that a gun, chance-met among a stranger's clutter, was embraced as her last viable option?

My heart was pounding as if I'd been running for some long, uphill time. My brain, panting, put forth the notion that perhaps—perhaps the body at the Mill hadn't been Lisa's at all and for a moment I was lightheaded, almost weeping with joy, because of *course—*

Common sense reasserted itself. ID had been obtained from the Mill's manager, corroborated by the cleaning crew shift boss, solidified by the driver's license tucked into the back pocket of her jeans. Lisa Gagnon was dead of a gunshot wound to the head, no mistake.

But she hadn't–she couldn't have–shot herself.

I put the Camaro into gear, drifted down to the edge of the lot, looked both ways along 201 and pulled out, heading south.

*

If you take the Back Road out of Skowhegan, you run into Route 104, which brings you into Wimsy along the River Road, 'way across town from Wimsy Point.

Which is as good a reason as I can give for taking the left onto the Winding Hill Road and then the next left, down to Fox's place.

The new key slid in smooth and the old lock turned like butter. I stepped into the stone-floored foyer, groped briefly for the switch and swung the door shut as the electric candles glowed to life.

I slipped my key ring into a pocket, shook the snow off the parka and hung it on a peg before proceeding to the Salon. A snap of the switch revived the dusty chandelier and I stepped up to the corner cabinet hardware repository which was the least part of the phenomenon known as *Random Access*.

I pirated an unmarked disk from a mostly-full box on the cluttered table, and slid it into the A drive.

The screen displayed a shifting "Waiting for Caller" notice. I touched a key, got the home menu, dropped the cursor to "Sysop" and typed in the password. The screen flicked, displaying the top-secret system operator menu, from which vantage I could, if the mood was on me, work inestimable mischief of which unilaterally changing everyone's password, blitzing the message base and corrupting the file library was only the beginning.

Slowly, double-checking my choices before I toggled them so I wouldn't inadvertently kill a user file or so much as a single message, I asked the board to check the A drive. It did so, assuring me that the disk it found there was formatted, empty and ready to take data. I then asked it to make an archive of all messages sent by Lisa Gagnon and send that file to disk.

The computer beeped, accepting the task, and produced various whirs and clicks as the drives worked. Eventually, there was another beep and a message stating that compilation of "Lisa.txt" was concluded. Did I wish to view the file?

I touched "Y"; enter.

I'd known Lisa for an avid correspondent, but as a general user, I'd only seen the tip of the iceberg. The first letter in the file names itself first of 313 messages, and further elucidated that 176 of the 313 were private messages to other users, though "private" never is on an electronic bulletin board, where nothing is hidden from the sysop's godlike eye.

Feeling cold, cramped and anything but godlike, I pursued Lisa Gagnon down 313 messages, written, you might say, on air; insubstantial, except for those who possessed the modern version of the camera obscura—the computer—and the particular, peculiar urge to connect in the non-world of cyberspace.

We're all ghosts in the machine—the ones of us who travel by modem. We're all timeless, no more alive, and no less, than Lisa was now—until the sysop deletes our messages.

Three hundred and thirteen messages later, I closed the file and tucked it into the Sysop's private cubbyhole, then put *Random Access* back on line. The machine ran a self-check and declared itself awaiting callers. I closed my eyes and just—stood there.

The woman revealed by the messages wasn't a rocket scientist: She was opinionated, frequently silly, practical, resilient—even optimistic—in the face of a small squadron of life's nastier setbacks. Her messages did not scintillate, but they did carry that indefinable, invaluable, flavor of *caring*, of *interest*, so vital to satisfying electronic conversation.

Guns were not mentioned overmuch in her conversations—except for three or four rather heated private exchanges with Mark Bernier—but when they were, they were mentioned with loathing.

What would make a gun-phobe shoot herself? The world is full of the means to take one's own life—from drinking Drano to leaping into the Smoke; from sleeping pills to bridge abutments.

And there was still the question of—why.

Why is the burden of every survivor: Why her and not me? Why now? Why didn't I see? Why didn't I help? *Why did she do it?*

Why.

I rubbed my eyes and opened them, staring at the Waiting for Caller screen, but seeing Dan Skat's photo: the blood-soaked rug, the spattered wall, the ruined, crumbled shape of a woman . . .

Lisa *couldn't* have shot herself. Not tonight. Not ever.

Which meant someone else had.

I swallowed and closed my eyes again, while my brain added *who* to *why*.

Abruptly, I shivered, though I'd been warm a moment before, and opened my eyes in time to see the waiting screen flicker and change.

Ring detected, *Random Access* told me, and the screen flickered again, while the status bar registered a connection of 19200, commonly called nineteen-two, and which is geek-speak for "pretty damn' fast."

The Welcome screen flicked into being and was banished immediately. *Random Access* requested name and password and the letters snapped onto the screen like a conjuror's trick:

David E. Foxwell, followed by a row of dots

representing his password.

I reached out and stood there with my hand over the keys while the board ushered him in. When the Main Menu solidified, I touched the Alt key, then C.

Main Menu vanished; the screen displayed the familiar Chat field. The first message was from Fox–*under* the line, which threw me for a moment, until it I remembered that our roles were indeed reversed.

Jennifer?

My fingers moved, quickly: ***I know what time it is.***

All right, Fox typed equitably. ***Did the board crash?***

No. I stared at the screen, trying to think of the best way to tell him. While I was thinking, my fingers moved again. ***Fox, where are you?***

In an extremely bland and boring hotel in Arlington, Virginia. I have only just returned from surveying the damage. Mr. Wylie's done quite a job of baking his system. Really, I'm impressed. There was a slight pause–too slight, thank God, for my fingers to start up again on their own.

It looks like I'm stuck here for the week, by the time I write new code and reconfigure the system. Another pause; I had the impression of a sigh. ***I hesitate to say that the new incarnation will be foolproof, as inventive as Mr. Wylie has proven himself. But I'm going to make it much harder for him next time. Not to mention raising my hourly.***

I blinked, my fingers quiet on the keypad. In a moment, more words appeared on Fox's side of line.

What's happened, Jennifer?

My fingers moved, slow now that they had to give the news. ***Lisa's dead. Lisa Gagnon.***

The pause this time was long–so long that my fretful ***Fox?*** and his stunned ***How?*** hit the screen simultaneously.

I gulped, feeling tears burning the back of my eyes, now that I had someone else– someone else who *knew*–to talk to.

She was shot. At work. The cops think suicide.

That's ridiculous. His response was immediate. Then: *Did Bill send yo—*

It was my shift, my fingers interrupted with a clatter. Fox stopped in the middle of a word, then deliberately spaced down a line.

Yes, he typed. And added two more lines. ***Thinking.***

I came here, my fingers told him, garrulous again, *to check the board—all that stuff she wrote about guns and how much she hated them —she COULDN'T have shot herself!* I wailed, the screen suddenly blurring as the tears brimmed.

No, of course she couldn't have, Fox typed gently. ***The police will figure that out—have probably already figured it out. Jennifer—*** He stopped typing.

I used the back of my hand to scrub the damn' tears away and touched the keyboard again. ***Here.***

Yes, he agreed, and then nothing else, though the screen displayed a slow series of periods—"think dots"—to show me that we were still connected; that he was ordering his thoughts before typing again. I gulped, found a Kleenex in my pocket and did a more thorough mop-up.

Jennifer, I know it's your shift and your story . . . The words, when they came, came slowly. ***. . . but don't do anything . . . rash, will you? If . . . you can stay there—at my place . . . if you like.***

I have to feed Jasper, my fingers objected. Once again, I received the impression of a sigh from Fox's side before his answer appeared.

Indeed you do. Jasper is, however, a gentleman. If he consents to being relocated, I don't object to him being there with you, if you want to stay.

I left my parents' house when I was eighteen, married when I was nineteen, divorced when I was twenty. My parents are dead; my sister gave up worrying about me years ago, if she ever had. Which is fine. I can take care of myself.

But Fox was worried. About *me*, specifically. That got me somewhere in the mid-gut and I bit my lip, suddenly remembering my early-evening conversation with Bill Jacques. Remembering that Fox's wife had been murdered; remembering that it had been Fox who came to fetch me from the hospital the night the man with the gun tried to kill me. The night I wrecked my car.

Jennifer?

I brought my fingers down lightly on the keys. *Thinking,* I told him. *And what I think is that I'll be OK. Most people who are ... murdered—it's personal, between them and someone else. I'm just a reporter. I'm doing my job. Covering my shift.* I paused, stringing a line of think dots with my index finger.

... I think I'll be OK at home, I repeated.

A pause, longish.

All right. The offer stands. If anything changes.

OK, I answered, eyes filling again. *Thank you, Fox.*

You're welcome, he told me, then more brusquely, the words appearing on the screen simultaneously: *Get a pen and paper. I'll give you some phone numbers.*

I found a pen among the clutter beside the monitor, tore a page off a tablet I found on the shelf holding the CPU. By the time I had cleared a corner so I could write, there were three Arlington area phone numbers on the screen, each with its designator: Hotel, Wylie's Private Line, Receptionist. I dutifully copied them down, glanced back to the screen and saw a fourth number had been added to the list, this one preceded not by area code 703, but an unfamiliar 512. As I watched, words formed: *Vulpine Cybernetics, Austin, Texas.*

Pen over paper, I stared at the screen. Fox is—most recently—from Austin, Texas. Kathy Foxwell had died in Austin, Texas. I lay the pen down and touched the keyboard: *?*

*My—company—*Fox typed slowly. *If you can't find me at any of the other numbers, call VCS and leave a message with Geena or Nelson ... I'll also check here for messages. OK?*

OK, I typed agreeably, and copied down the last

number, though it was just as silly as copying down the rest. What was Fox going to do from Virginia, if I found trouble in Wimsy? Still, if it made him feel better . . .

All set, I told him, and sighed, abruptly and entirely exhausted. **I'm going close things up here and go on home now. Thank you, Fox. I'm glad you called.**

I'm glad I called, too, he answered. **Be careful, Jennifer. Remember to lock your door.**

I'll remember, I promised, folding the phone numbers into my pocket. **CYA.**

Sleep well, Fox wished me, and I hit the toggle that released him into the board.

16

"A hotel maid." Jerry's voice was loud, like he thought maybe I was deaf. Or Bill was. It was also flatly disbelieving. He rattled this morning's front page and glared at us both while John lounged against the corner of the desk, looking amused.

"A local resident, a violent death," Bill said from beside me, his voice coolly polite. "That's news, Mr. Talbot."

"OK, it's news," Jerry snapped. "But *front page* news?"

"It's a small town, Mr. Talbot," Bill said patiently while I concentrated on keeping my seat without screaming or throwing things.

Jerry sighed sharply, and shook the paper again.

"All right, then," he said, in viscous mimicry of Bill's patience. "Some local yokel decides to blow her brains out and it's front page news. Great. You're the editor, Mr. Jacques. I bow to your expertise. Now, you want to tell me *why* she did it–*Ms. Pierce?*"

I met his glare. "The cops don't know and Lisa wasn't talking," I told him, voice shaking with combined exhaustion and fury. "I'm a *reporter*, Mr. Talbot. I only write down what people tell me."

"Sounds to me like you're a stenographer," John drawled.

I caught myself before I answered–just–and took another deep breath, refusing to either take the bait or meet his eyes. *Hang on, Jen. This is not a good day to lose your job.*

The silence stretched. I ground my teeth together and stared at my hands, knotted and white-knuckled against my denimed knee.

"Nothing to say, Ms. Pierce?" That was Jerry. I lifted my head and caught him with the smirk full on his face. I turned to Bill.

"I'm going over to the police station and see if they've got anything new," I told him, talking out the scope of the story, editor to reporter, just like the Twins were in Albuquerque still and not glowering at us from less than two feet away. "What else?"

Bill turned in his chair, giving me his face and the Talbots his shoulder. "You know the drill—talk with the family, friends, co-workers. Fill in her background—we were pretty sketchy last night—Wimsy native?"

I shook my head, remembering information from an electronic letter never meant for my eyes. "Grew up in Cornville, dropped out of Skowhegan High. Moved to Wimsy to be closer to her job." I sighed. "She was laid off from Welltread a couple months ago."

"That's the stuff we want," Bill said approvingly. "Solid, local stuff. Augusta News'll play up the blood-and-guts. We want *her*. We want the reactions of the people who knew her." He nodded, to himself I thought, then looked at me hard. "If anybody wants to speculate on *why*, that's speculation and that's how it runs."

This was standard operating procedure, Jacques-style. I nodded. "Sure."

"OK, then. We're looking at top of page two—maybe a jump inside from one, depending on what you get. Take the extra camera, in case you need to grab a shot. If they're OK with it, schedule a time for Dan to go by and do a formal."

"Right."

"Anything else on your plate?" Bill asked.

"I'm supposed to talk to Bert Gantry about the new addition to his studio." Bert Gantry is Wimsy's resident artist and self-proclaimed Renaissance Man. Anything that takes place in his life is, by Bert's definition, news. Bill sighed.

"Milt'll take that one. You stick with Lisa—OK?"

"OK," I said, and stood, feeling better—steadier—than I had in many hours. I pushed myself to my feet.

"Check in before you call it a day," Bill said. I nodded and turned to go, catching sight of The Twins as I did. Jerry had lowered the front page to his desk and was sitting with his hands folded atop the newsprint. John had gone rigid, and his arms were folded tightly across his chest. Both baby-skinned faces held an identical look of disbelieving outrage.

I paused and tipped my head, catching Jerry's eye on mine.

"Nothing to say, Mr. Talbot?" I asked sweetly–and swept out into the hallway.

*

Gene the dispatcher looked up from his paperwork as I came through the gate.

"Sergeant's tied up."

"Oh." I checked. "Will he be long, do you think?"

He shrugged.

Right. "Anybody else around who can talk to me about the death at–"

"Could try the Chief."

Well, I supposed I could, at that. I nodded to Gene. "Thanks."

"Ayuh."

Chief Twitchell's office is on the second floor of the police station-fire department building. I turned left out of the main station, heading for the stairs at the end of the short hallway.

"And I'm telling *you*, she *hated* guns!" The man was bellowing rather than yelling, like an animal in pain. I stopped in my tracks and turned to stare at the door that had failed to contain his anguish. *Sergeant*, read the imitation brass tag.

There was a momentary silence, or maybe John Therriault answered, low enough to be muffled by the door.

"What the hell's the matter with you–you deaf?" The sound hurt *my* ears, buffered as I was. Deafness wasn't John's present problem, but it might well be in his future.

"She hated guns, you understand that? Said they made her sick. Had me sell my rifles before we got married–'Them or me'–that's what she told me and she meant it, too. Wouldn't go to her own brother's birthday party because there was guns in the house. And now you're trying to say she *shot* herself? *It ain't possible*, you listening to me?"

The entire town would be listening to him in a second. I took an involuntary step backward, which was a good thing, because the bellowing resumed and this time he was *really* loud, like maybe John had started to say something he'd rather not hear.

"Listen, I don't care what kind of cover-up you're trying to pull, but by Jesus you better get offa your lazy cop butt and find out who killed my wife!"

There was a bang then, and an echoing metallic boom– smacked the gunmetal gray municipal desk a good one, I thought–then the door snapped open and he was out into the hallway, moving fast.

Through the open door, I saw John Therriault, standing rigid in the center of his tiny office, hands fisted at his sides.

I turned and ran up the hall.

*

I caught him in the parking lot–a broad guy in a red-and-black chamois shirt open over a black T-shirt, shorter than me, but quick on his legs–I was panting by the time I made his side.

"Mr. Gagnon? You have a minute . . . ?" He stopped. Turned to stare: Dark brown eyes, slightly protuberant and shiny-wet; thick black eyebrows, arched high like a woman's. I shook my head, wheezing, and groped in my pocketbook for a card.

"Jen Pierce," I told him, handing over a beige rectangle. "From the *Voice*."

He took the card, didn't look at it; stuffed it in a pocket.

"Yeah?" The stare had become a glare, the wet brown eyes were rimmed with red.

"I'd like to talk to you about Lisa," I said.   "For the paper."

"Paper wants a story, does it?" His voice in non-bellow was deep, a oddly comforting, craggy rumble. He leaned forward, shoving one finger at my nose. "I'll give you a story: She didn't shoot herself." The eyes dared me to deny it.

"I know," I said, then shivered as the wind gusted across the parking lot. "Look, can I buy you a cup of coffee?"

He blinked, then grabbed my arm and turned toward Main Street, which I took for "yes," and four minutes later we were sitting among the foliage and Micky dispatched for a mug of Swiss-chocolate-almond and another of French Roast, that being the closest to "just gimme a cupa coffee–strong, black and sweet" in Michaelson's inventory.

The coffee arrived like a conjuring trick. Dan Gagnon picked up four bags of turbinado sugar from the white china serving plate, ripped their heads off and dumped the contents into his mug. So much for "sweet. "

I poured cream, set the pitcher aside and looked up to find him staring at me.

"So how come the *Voice* knows what the cops say they don't?"

I shook my head. "The *Voice* doesn't know it," I told him. "But I've–heard–Lisa talk about guns, and I have a hard time believing she shot herself. *Personally.*" I stressed the last word.

He gave that a few seconds of thought before picking up his spoon and clanging it around inside his mug.

"Yah," he allowed. "OK. So what do you want from me?"

"Tell me about Lisa–about you and Lisa. Tell me why you think she didn't shoot herself." I sipped my coffee cautiously, then looked back at him. "Tell me what the cops said."

He sighed, sagging back in his chair like he'd sprung a leak. "Damn Johnny–we go all the way back to elementary school. Used to listen when you talked to him. Then."

"He's still sticking with the suicide idea, I take it."

Dan Gagnon hefted his mug and sat staring down into it. "Says there's a procedure. Says there's rules of evidence. Says the evidence so far points to she shot herself." He looked up. "Which is bullshit–hell, you knew Lisa! I don't hafta tell you it's bullshit."

I put my notebook on the table, uncapped my pen. "Tell me anyway," I said–and he did. At length.

*

The Twins had gone home by the time I made it back to the newsroom, which was just as well. There's no deadline on Monday night, because there's no paper on Tuesday. Even Jack-the-Jock was gone.

Bill Jacques, however, was still at his desk. He looked at me over the top of his half-glasses when I dragged myself in, then took them off to look again.

"Ms. Pierce. We'd given you up."

I shook my head, too tired to glare. "Page one."

Bill put his glasses back. "Send it over when you're done."

*

At 10:30, I stopped typing, ran the spell checker, closed, saved, renamed and sent my story. Creakily, bad shoulder spitting curses, I got up and went over to lean my elbows on the top of Bill's monitor.

"Murder-point-Jen," I said, and my voice was creaky,

too. He flicked me a glance, looked down and touched keys.

"Got it," he said quietly, and, "It'll be a minute."

"I'm in no hurry," I told him and closed my eyes, the heat from the monitor vents warming my elbows and forearms.

The story I'd turned in was simple, merely a litany of the people who'd known Lisa, starting with her husband, proceeding to her sister, her mother, her favorite aunt, the brother whose birthday party she refused to attend, the girl who had stitched next to her on the bench at Welltread, the cleaning staff at The Mill–the people who known her, closely or not so. The people who said, to a man, that she'd never do it–not a *gun*. Not Lisa.

Nine people were quoted in the story. The ninth was John Therriault, who'd talked with me–patiently, professionally–about evidence and about the scene of the death, forensic data and the report of the officer responding to the call. I'd tried to talk to Ken Aube, too, but it was his off-shift, John said. I'd called Ken at home, but nobody answered the phone.

"OK," Bill said and I opened my eyes, looking at him blearily. "You didn't talk to the Chief?"

I shook my head. "Not around. Ken Aube's off today and nobody home when I called."

Bill nodded, looked down briefly and touched keys. "Get the Chief and Ken tomorrow–it'll go page one next issue."

Next issue was Wednesday. I usually work nights on Tuesday–meeting night.

"Milt'll take the planning board," Bill said, as if he actually thought Milt *would*. "You stick with this one."

"You're the boss." I pushed myself upright and shook my head to clear it. Bill frowned.

"You need a ride?"

"I'll be OK. The car knows the way home."

I went back to my desk, picked up the jacket I'd flung over Sue Danforth's monitor and shrugged it on. I gathered up the rest of my stuff and headed for the door.

"See you tomorrow," I said as I passed Bill's desk.

"I'll be here." He reached up to snap off his desk lamp.

17

Ken Aube lived on Elm Street, two narrow, short-lawned houses up from the corner of Pine. I'd been there once before, to interview Ken about his volunteer work for the Franco-American Club's Youth Program. There'd been an Escort that had seen better days in the driveway then, and the tiny backyard had been overrun with kids from the program, enjoying the August afternoon, the picnic, and each other.

A new blue Ford pickup bulked in the drive that separated Ken's house from the house on its right. I parked at the curb, walked back to where the drive entered the street and followed it up to the neatly shoveled sidewalk, my shoulder brushing the side of the truck. Breath frosting in the two-degree air, I climbed eight steep wooden steps to the porch.

The storm door was white aluminum with a scalloped cut-out framing the single window. Behind it was a blonde wood door with six thin panes set in a diagonal line from the hinge side to the knob. In the shadow between the doors, the panes looked black. Opaque.

An imitation mother-of-pearl button glowed faintly in the door-frame. I thumbed it, and a *ding-dong* straight out of *I Love Lucy* yodeled inside the house, plainly audible through the doors.

The yodel died away, leaving me standing on the porch surrounded by the fog of my own breath.

I sighed, to the increase of the fog bank, and thumbed the button again.

This time, in the bell's aftermath, I heard a measured boom from inside the house, growing progressively louder. I took a breath, swallowing fog, and the wooden door jerked open with the sucking noise of disrupted vacuum.

Ken Aube frowned at me while the scalloped storm-window grew frost flowers, then pushed the storm door open.

"What?"

Not the most gracious greeting I've ever had—or the rudest. "I'd like to talk to you about the murder, if you've got a few minutes."

His face flickered, going from annoyed to bland like somebody'd hit the remote.

"What murder?"

I gave him my best round-eyed, chiding look. "Lisa Gagnon."

Ken sighed, gusting out a small storm of frost, and suddenly shoved the storm door wider. "Come in here, will you? I don't feel like heating the whole damn street."

Gratefully, I slithered past him and stood in the hallway while he shut both doors and turned, crooking an irritable finger. "This way," he said and went down the hall ahead of me, floorboards booming beneath him.

The hallway ran the length of the house, with the stairway rising on the left. I flicked a glance into the living room as I went by: leather-and-chrome recliner strategically situated before chrome-and-glass entertainment center, shelves lined with video boxes, a newspaper open on the glass topped coffee table in front of the black leather couch. Everything looking crisp, newish and ordinary.

Which surprises you, why? I asked myself, following Ken down the hall, past two closed doors and into the kitchen. Ken walked over to the table, picked a mug up from among the other dishes and took a swig. Three steps into the kitchen, I stopped, blinking in the fluorescent light. It was a nice kitchen, the whole width of the house, with half-bricked walls, a modern range and hood, a dishwasher and a granite-topped counter. The floor was slate and a thermal glass slider overlooked a thin deck and narrow back yard. Definitely an upgrade since the last time I'd been here.

"Hey, this is great," I said and Ken turned, face cop-bland. He looked around briefly, like he was seeing the room for the first time, then shrugged.

"I've been fixing the place up," he said, raised his mug–then stopped, face thawing slightly. "Coffee?"

"Coffee'd be good, thanks."

He nodded, strode over to the bank of cherry wood cabinets, jerked open a door and extracted a mug, which he filled from the coffeemaker by the microwave. He slid a jar of coffee whitener, a sugar bowl and a spoon forward and topped off his mug, not bothering with either. I stepped up and added some whitener to my mug, and took a cautious sip. Coffee to put some hair on your chest, yessir! Whether you wanted it or not.

Ken leaned a hip against the counter and looked at me, one arm folded across his chest, the other bent at the elbow, coffee mug at the ready.

"OK, Jen, what's going on?"

I had another sip of memorable coffee and put the mug carefully on the counter.

"Like I said, I'd like to talk to you about Lisa Gagnon's murder," I said, and pulled the notebook out of my pocket.

Ken shook his head. "That's no murder. That's suicide."

I gave him another round-eyed look. "Family says murder. All her friends say murder."

"Yeah." He took a swig of coffee. "The state cops say suicide, Jenny. Families been wrong before."

True enough. But– "There's a problem with this suicide."

Ken sighed, and his face softened a little. "There's always a problem with a suicide. Family, friends–they all ask *why*. They all say she had everything to live for. They all say there has to be some mistake–it has to be someone else did them. Because otherwise, see, it's the family's fault–and nobody wants to live with that." Another gulp of coffee before he met my eyes, bleakly.

"So it's the cops' fault–the cops are lazy, they say. The cops want to close the case." He banged the mug to the counter, and I winced for the granite. "The fucking cops just don't give a shit."

Which was pretty much what they had said, in their own way. Except . . .

"Look, Jen, you talk to the Chief?"

"I couldn't catch him yesterday," I said. "I'm going to try again today."

"Yeah, well, he's the one you want to talk to–medical examiner, state boys–hell, you know what you're doing. What I did, I answered the call. I secured the scene. I called for backup. We got a procedure–the Chief can tell you all about it."

In fact, John Therriault had told me all about it yesterday, but it didn't seem worth mentioning at the moment. I sighed slightly and slipped the notebook into my pocket.

"Sorry to have disturbed your breakfast," I said.

He straightened up and came forward, friendly, now that I was going to be out of his hair.

"Hey, no problem. You got a job, I got a job. We both do our jobs, right? Maybe not everybody's happy, but we get by."

This homily got us out of the kitchen and down the hall to the front door. I stood back, and Ken put his hand on the knob. He pulled the door open and I stepped forward, put my hand on the storm door's latch, then turned and looked back, catching his eyes.

"Say, Ken?"

He sighed. "Yeah?"

"I don't want to get you in trouble or anything, but, about your securing the room . . ."

He didn't say anything, just watched me, his face so bland my cheekbones ached in sympathy.

"See, I talked to somebody who got past the cops downstairs somehow, and had a look into that room. They said there wasn't anybody on the door."

Ken shook his head. "What? They get pictures? They got proof?" He reached past me and pushed the latch, shoving the storm door open a bit. "You can't believe everything you hear, Jen. See you."

I searched his face, much good it did me, then dredged up a smile and nod. "Thanks!" I said, and stepped out onto the porch.

I was three steps down when I heard the doors shut behind me, one after the other.

*

Chief Twitchell is big. He's also loud, having come up the runt, as he told me once, among four older and louder brothers. "You learned to speak up or you starved," he'd boomed good-naturedly.

He was booming now, palpably patient, and not likely to stay that way long, if I was any judge of the matter.

"I've talked with the sister, which I guess you have, too," he said, cheeks Cortland apple red. I nodded.

He sighed. "The sister's upset," he said, which was fair enough. "The mother's upset. The—what? husband? ex?–he's upset. They're all upset—and they've got a right to be upset. They've got a right to know that the investigation is proceeding along proper lines. They've got a right to raise concerns." He lifted a big hand and pointed a forefinger the size of a pepperoni in my direction.

"What they don't have is the right to tell us how to do our job. And they sure don't have a right to tell us it was murder when everything we've got says suicide. I'm sorry for the family, but this department knows its work. If there was any little question about it being the other way–but there isn't. It was suicide." He shook his head, lines harsh around his mouth. "God knows, I'd rather it'd never happened at all. We don't always get our rathers."

We damn' seldom get our rathers, in my experience, but I didn't bring that up. Instead, I looked down at the notebook and fluttered some pages, nodding to myself as if I were quick-checking my notes.

"So you talked to the hotel guest," I said, looking up from my fluttering.

He frowned. "Hotel guest."

"The person who was staying in the room where Lisa was . . . where they found Lisa. The person whose gun–"

"Dwight Alexander," the Chief interrupted me.

"Right," I said, like I'd heard the name before, looked down and made a note. Eyes still on the pad, I asked, "Where is he now?"

There was a pause, thunderous in its silence. I looked up.

Chief Twitchell had reached the edge of his patience, judging by the increased flame of his cheeks. He took a long breath and met my eyes.

"He checked out," he stated, perfectly even.

"OK," I said, making a note.

"Sunday night," the Chief finished, the boom in monotone.

I blinked. "You let him go that soon? Suicide was that obvious–" Chief Twitchell raised a hand, showing me a palm the size of Rhode Island. I stopped.

"We didn't get a chance to talk to him," he said. "Apparently all the ruckus spooked him and he took his rental car and drove off. Left quite a few of his things in the room. We're looking for him. It's irregular, I grant you. But it doesn't make that suicide a murder, Jenny."

"Right," I said, and it sounded caustic to me. I flipped the notebook closed and stood. "Thanks."

"No problem," he said, standing and holding out a hand. "Facts aren't always easy on the gut."

I put my hand in his and shook, my stomach tight.

"No," I managed. "They sure aren't."

*

The Mill's parking lot was almost empty, mid-morning of a Wednesday. I pulled in close and walked briskly across the clean-plowed blacktop, heading for the front doors.

Once inside, I went straight, then left past the elevators. A short hallway opened abruptly into a garden—benches and double-chairs cunningly tucked among foliage that would expire upon two minutes exposure to a typical Maine *summer*. The floor was flagstone—imitation garden path—and arched slightly as it crossed a frothing artificial stream on its way downroom to power the model waterwheel.

The garden benches were empty, though I did spot a guy with a maid's cart, far back, apparently emptying ashtrays.

Just the other side of the bridge, the main path went right. I followed it to a structure that looked a great deal like a hotel's front desk masquerading as an open-sided rustic shelter. The inside of the shelter was lit by spots; telephones, credit card machines and a computer were strategically placed along the low counter. A gray-haired man in a Ragg wool sweater was pecking at the computer keyboard, a frown bracketing his precise gray mustache.

"Hi," I said.

He glanced up, frown smoothing away into pleasant professional blandness.

"Mr. McElroy?" I said. Pleasant blandness gave way to pleasant puzzlement.

"That's right," he said and I stuck my hand out.

"Jennifer Pierce, from the *Voice*."

"Of course." He smiled, the professional host, and met my hand heartily. "How are you today?"

"Pretty well," I said, which was not specifically true, but why muddy the waters with the truth? "I wonder if you might have a couple minutes to talk with me." I smiled. "I was here last night—but I missed you."

He shrugged, and a hint of sorrow was allowed to touch his face. "The police did monopolize my time last night," he said, with no noticeable sarcasm. "I'll be happy to answer your questions, if you don't mind asking them here—my day manager called in sick and I'm covering."

"This is fine," I told him, pulling out the notebook and pen. He eyed them with a shade more apprehension than an ordinary blue Bic and a battered steno book should have occasioned.

"Of course, I didn't know Lisa very well," he said, without waiting for me to uncap the pen. "She'd only worked here a short time before...well. She was a good employee—" he smiled, slightly "—that Maine work ethic—eager to pitch in, eager to learn. No job was beneath her." He shrugged again, eyes on the pen as I guided it through some pothooks and whatnots. "She was a likable person. I liked her. I believe everyone here liked her. She always seemed cheerful—happy—and she was off to a very good start in her employment. I'm sure I had no idea . . ." He let that fade off, eyes still on the pen.

"You take shorthand," he said, with a certain wonder in his voice. "I haven't seen someone take shorthand in twenty years."

Twenty years ago, I'd been sitting in a classroom at Parkville Senior High School, blue Bic gripped in sweaty fingers, taking timed dictation at 40, 50 and 60 words a minute and wishing I'd opted for the college prep course. The year after I graduated, shorthand was cut from the business curriculum.

"A dead art," I agreed with Grant McElroy. "Comes in handy, though."

"I expect it must," he said and managed, finally, to move his eyes from my notes and back to my face. "Is there anything else you'd like to know, that I might know? She worked here for such a—"

"I do have one more question," I said, cutting him off before he could start the official tape again. He blinked.

"I wonder," I continued, "if you can tell me anything

about the person whose room it was. It would be helpful if I could see the register, but if that's against the rules . . ." I let it drift off and smiled as winningly as I knew how.

Grant McElroy returned the smile, and this time actual human malice showed. "Mr. Alexander arrived Sunday afternoon. I assume that he departed sometime Sunday evening–he did not pay us the courtesy of checking out." Malice faded and he sighed.

"I wish I could show you the register, but–" He reached over and patted the computer. "We've got the whole check-in and out system computerized and–I'm afraid we had a meltdown–our computer's at the Central Processing Unit. This is the spare." He sighed again. "I hope our machine will be back tomorrow."

I digested this in silence, trying to keep a rein on the frustration.

"You'd have backups, though, right?" I asked eventually. Mr. McElroy looked stern.

"We *should* have backups," he said austerely. "However, it appears that–some people–have not been–precise–in following the routine."

And some people, I inferred, were in an ocean of extremely warm water. Well, damn.

I capped the pen and flicked the notebook closed, giving Grant McElroy one last smile as I extended my hand.

"Thank you very much for your time."

"My pleasure," he said, affable mask back in place. "If there's anything else I can do . . ."

"I'll give you a call," I promised, and made my way out of the garden.

*

Carl pointed. "There she is, and melt down she did. We ain't gettin' no files back off that baby."

"She" was a perfectly ordinary-looking cream-colored

desktop CPU with a five-and-a-quarter-inch disk drive and a three-and-a-half-inch ditto. I sighed and looked back to Carl.

"What happened?"

He shrugged. "Virus, looks like. Nasty one. Overwrote the whole hard drive with zeros."

This was pretty standard—so standard that a bright boy or girl somewhere in the wilds of Silicon Valley had gimmicked a fix whereby the overwriting zeros were carefully *un*overwritten, and the original data made retrievable. Pretty clever solution, that was.

But not clever enough.

Goaded, the virus-builders devised a two-stage approach: One, you overwrite the hard drive with zeros.

Two. You delete the zeros.

After this treatment, little bitty pieces of the original data will, theoretically, still be floating about in the blasted landscape of the hard. Theoretically—if you're patient, desperate or Really Good—those bits of original data can be netted and painstakingly fitted back into something approaching a whole.

Most people just cut their loses and install a new hard drive.

"So you can recover the files, right?" I asked Carl. He shook his head.

"This one did the Memphis Two-Step. I ain't gonna try piecing together what's left. Fox might be able to do it, if Mr. Boston wants to fork over couple bills an hour to pay for his time." He wrinkled his nose. "Bunch of room reservations—how important can it be? Cheaper to replace the drive and pay the bookkeeper overtime to go through the charge slips and noodle out the winnings."

Reasonable advice—practical and cost-effective. Except—

"Fox charges *two hundred dollars an hour* for his time?"

Carl's eyebrows pulled together. He rubbed one finger along the side of his nose.

"Might be more," he allowed, after a minute. "Fox is wicked big mojo."

In fact, Lord Fox of Cyberspace, by order of the Council of Virtual Knights, who, despite their rather peculiar take on everyday reality, do not award such honors lightly. Lord Fox had won his place in a strange and competitive–not to say cutthroat–land and Lord Fox could charge what the market would bear–or not–at his discretion. Certainly, the Town of Wimsy had never ponied up that kind of money to get the police computers on-line–which rather disturbing thought I filed away for later examination.

"Right," I said, and sighed. The sleepless night was catching up with me–my eyes burned and I felt the shadowy clench of a headache just behind my forehead.

"So, what are you going to do with the computer?"

"Call Mr. Boston and tell 'im what I told you. Then I'll most likely pull the drive, drop in a new one and schlepp the whole pot roast back out to the Mill. Unless, like I said, he wants to rent Fox's brain."

Which he probably wouldn't want to do, and which was only sensible, all things considered. Which likewise meant Dwight Alexander was a dead-end and what was I doing here, anyway? The cops said Lisa committed suicide. The cops said Dwight Alexander was non-standard, and likely interesting for his own self, but not, by all the evidence they held, a murderer. End of the line. End of the story. *Go back to the newsroom and finish your story, Jen. Then get the heck to bed . . .*

"Jen?" That was Carl, sounding concerned.

I opened my eyes and shook my head, trying for a smile. "Sorry 'bout that." I hesitated, gauging him, "Do me a favor?"

He moved his shoulders fractionally. "Let's hear it."

"Save that hard drive for me."

Another shrug. "It'll cost you salvage."

"That's OK."

"It's yours, then." Far within his beard, he grinned. "Don't guess Fox'll charge you two bills an hour."

I blinked. "Look, Carl–"

The phone rang just then and he turned to answer it. After a second, it occurred to me that arguing the point was probably worse than ignoring it, so I waved at him and left.

18

The trouble with early to bed is the early to rise at the other end. I simultaneously fell into bed and unconsciousness at 6:14 Tuesday afternoon.

Five o'clock Wednesday morning I woke, alert and feeling positively well, with no smallest inclination to roll over and sleep some more.

That being the case, I rose, and had a leisurely, lavender-scented shower, towel-dried and combed my hair. I pulled on jeans, buttoned, but did not tuck in a thick old red plaid flannel shirt, shoved my feet into house moccasins and headed for the kitchen.

I'd make coffee, I thought as I skipped downstairs. Then I'd call *Random Access* and do my sysoply duties, which had gone untended last evening, then maybe I'd scramble a couple eggs for breakfast.

These thoughts revolving comfortably in my head, I snapped on the kitchen light and rummaged the coffee can out of the depths of the fridge. At the counter, I pulled the coffee maker forward, slid the grounds basket out and–

There was a knock at the door.

I jumped, basket clattering out of my hand and onto the counter top.

"Honestly, Jen," I muttered, then crossed the kitchen, flicked on the porch light and pulled open the door.

"You could at least look out the window first," Fox said pettishly.

"I thought it was Harry," I snapped back, which wasn't precisely true, because I'd've *heard* Harry's truck. "What're you doing here, anyway? It's not even dawn."

"And I'm demonstrably not Harry," he said, still cranky.

"The light was on."

True enough. But my house sits well down at the end of a longish drive. Even in bare-leafed winter light from my kitchen doesn't reach the Point Road, which is not exactly a main thoroughfare– it leads nowhere but down to the old ferry landing, and dead-ends at the edge of the river.

I was about to point these facts out when it occurred to me that Fox was *here* and he should have been in Virginia. And he was here *now*, at barely 6 a.m. Wednesday, which meant he'd caught a very late–or ridiculously early–flight, set down in Portland at 2:30 or 3, and then driven the two or so hours from Portland to Wimsy . . .

"For God's sake, you must be exhausted." I pulled the door wider. "I'm making coffee. Come in and have a cup."

Under the porch light, he hesitated, mouth tightening. "I–"

I sighed, loudly, and stepped back into the kitchen, holding the door wide. "*Now*, David."

One eyebrow went up, but he came inside meekly enough. "Thank you," he murmured. "I'd like a cup of coffee, Jennifer."

I closed the door and went back to the counter. After a moment, Fox went over to the pegs by the ell door and hung his parka up. By the time I'd finished with the coffee maker, he was standing in the middle of the kitchen, Jasper weaving a complex greeting dance around his ankles, tail at full salute.

"You made an impression," I said, grinning at him on my way to the fridge. Jasper has seen Fox just once before–on the night I wrecked my car.

I put the coffee can back on its shelf and looked over my shoulder. Fox was down on one knee, offering Jasper an introductory finger.

"Hungry?" I asked. He looked up, deep blue eyes– wary, I thought, or probably just tired. Light glittered red-gold along the points of an overnight beard. "I don't want to put you to any trouble."

I sighed. "We're past that part," I told him. "We're now at the top of the next page, right before I ask you what the hell you're doing here and what happened to Mr. Wiley."

The–wariness–eased a bit; he smiled his slender smile and came gracefully to his feet. "I am a little hungry, yes."

"Fine. I was going to scramble some eggs, anyway. I can throw in a couple more or you can–"

From outside came the sound of a serious metallic altercation, drawing implacably closer.

Fox's eyes widened and he spun on a heel, moving more quickly than I'd ever seen him move.

Outside, the altercation reached a crescendo and abruptly ceased. I closed the fridge and was halfway across the kitchen before the heavy steps banged up the wooden porch stairs: one, two, three. On 'three' I pulled open the door and stepped back.

"Morning, morning," said Harry Pelletier and stumped her way in, pink-and-white doughnut box secure in the crook of her arm.

"Good morning," I said, and closed the door. Harry took one more step and stopped, the better to stare at Fox, who was still poised on the balls of his feet in the middle of the kitchen, Jasper standing at attention beside him.

Harry stared at Fox. Fox stared at Harry. I was briefly tempted to lean back against the door and see who would break first, but Haroldene Pelletier is a stubborn woman and Fox is . . . Fox. A staring contest between the two of them might encompass days.

I cleared my throat.

"Harry, this is David Foxwell. Fox, this is Haroldene Pelletier."

Fox's eyebrows went up and he visibly relaxed. He was seen–as much as he was ever seen–to smile. "Harry, I'm extremely happy to meet you."

She gave him one of her gap-toothed grins then and nodded– "Likewise"–before stumping over to the table to lay her burden down, then over to the pegs, pulling her cap off as she went.

"Got a cup for me, Jen?"

"Got a cup for everybody, as soon as the machine finishes," I told her and went to the cabinet to haul down three mugs and three saucers. I looked over my shoulder at Fox.

"Milk's in the fridge."

He nodded and stepped over to that appliance. After some searching, I located the sugar bowl behind the toaster and carried it to the table with the saucers and three spoons, where Harry took charge and dealt them out, each spoon neatly atop a pink-and-white doughnut shop paper napkin.

I went back to the coffee maker, poured three mugs more or less full and set the pot back on the burner.

"I'll carry those," Fox said, virtually in my ear, but for a wonder I didn't jump, just turned my head to smile at him.

"Thanks."

Harry had the box open in the center of the table, contents displayed. The seductive aroma of fresh doughnut wafted from its depths.

"Good thing I brought a dozen," she said, accepting her mug from Fox.

"You *always* bring a dozen," I told her, sitting down.

"And wind up takin' ten of 'em home." She cocked an eye at Fox, who'd taken the chair to her right. "What d'you care to be called by?"

"Fox," he said, glancing up from pouring milk into his coffee.

"Fox it is, then," she said, separating a pink-filled pastry from the company of its fellows.

"You eatin' this morning, Jen?"

I took the milk from Fox and poured some into my mug. "I could be persuaded. How's the truck holding up?"

"Dubois knows his way 'round a vehicle," Harry said comfortably. "Fixed 'er up better'n new. Ain't had a minute's problem since." She took a bite of her doughnut. "Come by yesterday 'round supper-time, but you weren't home."

"Had to see a man about a gun." I chose a honey-dipped ring and pushed the box toward Fox. "And another one about a computer. Much good either did me."

"Computer?" That was Fox, who had taken a chocolate cruller from the box and broken it in half. "You didn't have a meltdown, did you, Jennifer?

I shook my head. "The Mill's reservation computer went belly-up. Carl says virus. He's going to recommend that they replace the drive. I asked him to keep the old one for me."

"Baked hard drives provide an exciting decorator accent for virtually every room in the house," he noted solemnly and dunked his doughnut.

Harry was spooning sugar into her mug. "Be able to fix it up, will you?"

"I don't want to fix it. I want to recover the data."

"There are more amusing things to do with a week or two of your life," Fox pointed out. "What's so wonderful about the data on a reservations computer?"

I looked at him. "The guy who was renting the room Lisa died in has vanished and she was killed with one of his guns."

He stared at me, mug momentarily arrested on its journey to his lips, then seemed to shake himself and took a sip.

"I'll look at it," he said.

I couldn't help myself. "There are more amusing things to do with a week or two of your life."

"Agreed. But I should be able to determine whether there's anything available for recovery in an hour or so." He took a bite of doughnut. "I can spare Lisa that much, I think."

I felt myself flush with irritation for my own pettiness and met his eyes. "Thanks."

"You're welcome. I'll pick the drive up from Carl this afternoon. Are you working this evening?"

"Off at five, theoretically."

"Then if you stop by my place around seven I should be able to tell you something. All right?"

I smiled at him. "Great."

"This is the girl shot herself at the Mill?" Harry was fishing her second–or was it her third?–sweet out of the box.

"The cops say she shot herself, but she was a gun-phobe," I told her. "Said it made her sick to be in the same room with a gun."

"Does make it seem peculiar she'd use a gun to die with," Harry said ruminatingly. "Though I remember Hodge Quinlan–so scared of heights he'd turn green if you had him three steps up a ladder. Killed himself–left a note explaining all about it." She paused to drink some coffee. "Took himself up to the top of the barn and jumped. Said in the note he was sick of living a coward and at least he'd die a hero." She shook her head and looked at me.

"Thing is, Jen, you can't tell what's going on in the mind of somebody who hurts that bad."

"I know that," I said, and cleared my throat. "But there are a few things that seem peculiar about this one–including that it seemed kind of . . . spur of the moment. No note, used a chance-met gun . . . I just– I'd just like to be sure, that's all."

"Can see that." Harry nodded.

Beside me, Fox put his mug down and pushed back his chair.

"I think I'd better go home and get some sleep," he told me. "Thank you for inviting me in, Jennifer." He glanced aside. "Harry, I'm very glad to have met you. Thank you for breakfast."

"That's all right. Take a couple with you for later."

"I'll pass," he told her, coming to his feet. "Leave mine with Jennifer."

Harry laughed. "Be careful on the roads."

"I will." He went to reclaim his parka. I finished my coffee and stood, moving toward the door.

"I'll see you this evening," Fox murmured.

"Seven," I said, opening the door for him. "I'll be there."

"Good. Lock the door." He was gone. I closed the door and dutifully engaged the latch before going back to the table with the pot and dividing the last of the coffee between my mug and Harry's.

"Thanks," she said, pulling the sugar bowl toward her. She slanted a wise eye in my direction. "I like your redhead."

I sighed and poured milk into my mug. "He's not *my* redhead."

"That's all right," said Harry, and chose another doughnut.

19

From nine to eleven I was on the Christmas Circuit—
that meant wandering around town, talking to men-women-
and-children-in-the-street about their holiday plans, and
checking in with local shopkeepers about seasonal sales thus
far. It would run below the fold on page one, and jump inside
to the list of Holiday Events being compiled by Features.

For the record, things were going pretty well for Wimsy
merchants.

Carl at the CPU reported himself up to his ears in
alligators—"Everybody wants a computer this year," he said,
and gave me a grin. "I ain't complainin'." Over at the Kraft
Korner, Karen allowed business to be a little slow—"Our busiest
season is between Halloween and Thanksgiving," she said.
"That's when people realize that, if they really intend to do
that counted cross-stitch for Christmas, they'd better get
crackin'. But we're selling a good number of kits, and yarn,
and such—for presents."

The Cinderella Shoppe was closed when I went by,
with a note in the window elucidating Winter Hours as Monday
through Friday noon to five, Saturday nine to two, Closed
Sunday.

Mother's Pantry, on the other hand, was open and
serving at least eight customers.

The bell jangled as I pushed the door open—and again
as I pushed it shut. The air smelled like cinnamon. There was
harp music on the stereo system, intermittently audible
between the babble of voices. I hesitated on the threshold,
not wanting to slow commerce. The stocky blond behind the
counter looked up, light glinting off her glasses, grinned and
waved me in.

"Step right up!" She called cheerfully, and moved to the right, leaving her staff to deal with the customers. I cut across the shop and met her at the back corner, out of the general crush.

"Hey," she said softly, crossing her arms on top the counter and resting her chin on her folded hands. "I'm glad you came by." Eliza Paul is a midwife, a Witch, a pro-Choice activist, and one of the driving forces behind Mother's Pantry Co-op. We get along. "Gaia Coven's throwing a Solstice party at Merry and Scott's and you're invited. Bring a friend, come alone, but be there or be square."

I grinned. "The twenty-second?"

"Right you are—we're supposed to start things off around eight, but don't let that bother you—come early, stay late."

"Pot luck?"

She shrugged. "Those of us who like to cook will bring goodies. Those of us who like to eat will bring appetites and appreciation."

"A fair division of labor."

"The fairest possible," she agreed.

"I'll try to be there," I said and thought that I would. My connection with The Craft, as the Pagan community calls itself, is tenuous, but Yule with Gaia Coven sounded—tempting.

"Try hard," Eliza told me and I nodded, pulling the pad and pen out of my pocket.

"Now that we've got the important stuff out of the way," I said, flipping pages, "the *Voice* wants to know how your Christmas season has been thus far."

"We've been right out straight," Eliza said. "Lots of people ordering in goodies for their various feasts, stopping by to pick up spices, specialty cheeses, teas—and then there's the orders for custom baked goods. I've got a bunch of Witches cooking up a storm." She cocked a blond eyebrow in my direction. "Figuratively, that is."

I grinned, made a note and flipped the book closed.

"Thanks," I said.

Eliza nodded, "Hang on a sec," she said, straightening and reaching behind the counter. There was a moment of rustling, then she was holding a white paper bag out to me. "Here you go," she said with a grin, "everybody's a winner."

"Thanks." I took the bag and unrolled the top, inhaling spicy sweetness and catching a glimpse of a gingerbread boy half-wrapped in bakery tissue. I rolled the top again and sent a look to Eliza. "How'd you know?"

She waggled her eyebrows and headed back toward the fray. "Know what?"

*

Back at the *Voice*, I had the newsroom to myself. According to the sheet, Bill Jacques and Milt were scheduled to come in at one; Carly and Sue at six. Dan Skat was out grabbing shots, and Features was dark. I turned on the scanner to keep me company, fired up the computer, and wrote my piece while snacking on gingerbread. When I was done, I went back to Features, made a pot of coffee, and hit the ladies room while it was dripping.

I carried my mug back to my desk and proofed the article in between sips, straightening out a couple of twisty sentences, and rewriting my lead in something more like the active voice. That done, I ran the spell-check, and sent the Thing Entire into the edit queue, wrote the name of the file on a sticky note and walked over to stick it with the rest of the happy crowd on the screen of Bill Jacques' computer: Sue's handwriting, Dan Skat's, Arlene from Features . . . Bill was going to be a busy man when he came in.

I squinted at the far wall. Quarter to one by the newsroom clock. Time for me to get my coat on again and head out to interview Darryl Pines at the Homeless Shelter.

*

You'd think that a town as small as Wimsy, Maine, wouldn't need a homeless shelter. You'd be wrong.

The Wimsy shelter is on High Street, in an old house that backs on to the IGA. The house had been left to the town some years back by Barbara Giguire, who had simply directed in her will that it be put to "good use." The Selectmen not having thought of an immediate "good use," the building languished until Darryl Pines came to them with a federal grant in his pocket and promises of help from various construction crews in the area.   You'd've thought that the town would've leapt at the chance to have a white elephant taken off their hands, brought up to code and kept there, and the Selectmen had been crystal clear on that particular benefit. But. There'd been some folks who didn't particularly want "those people" in their neighborhood, town–or, it seemed, planet.

Common decency–or the Selectmen's eagerness to be shut of the Giguire "gift"–did finally carry the day. It helped that Darryl Pines is a ruthless, golden-tongued son-of-a-gun who doesn't let anything stand between him and his goals. He has sworn, so he told me during the Open House, to use these powers only for good.

So far, he seems to be keeping his word.

The route to Darryl's office from the front door is down a long hall, turning left into what was once probably the parlor, but is now the activity room, straight to the door in the back wall. Behind the door is an office so cozy it barely accommodated Darryl, much less the overladen table that served as his desk and the small mountain range of files and paperwork.

On my previous visits the activity room had been empty. The Wimsy Shelter provides overnight accommodations only, and the guests had dispersed for the day by the time my customary late morning/early afternoon appointment rolled around.

This afternoon, Darryl was in the activity room with

what appeared to be three of the House's guests. A Christmas tree decorated with a construction paper chain and a thin string of twinkle lights stood in the corner next to the dark television. The group had drawn various donated chairs together in a clump and were involved in what appeared to be an intense conversation. One of the men—a thin guy with unruly black hair, wearing a gray cable knit sweater that had seen better days—was hunched forward in his chair, hands moving emphatically.

I hesitated in the door, not wanting to interrupt, but the lone women of the group saw me and announced loudly, "Mr. Pines, there's somebody here to see you, I bet."

Darryl got up from his chair, easy smile on his broad face, which meant nothing at all except that he was in Mr. PR Guy mode.

"Jen, thanks for coming."

"No problem," I said, walking into the room, and meeting his outstretched hand with my own. His was warm and slightly damp; his shake firm. When it was done, he introduced me to the others.

The woman was Bev; the guy in the gray cable-knit was Larry; and the other guy, an older man with a watch cap pushed back far enough to display the shine of a naked scalp, was Robert.

"We're just finishing up here," Darryl told me. "I wonder if I can ask you to wait in my office for a couple minutes?" He smiled winningly. "There's coffee."

I smiled back, though it was an effort; the conversation hadn't looked like it was in wind-down phase. On the other hand . . .

"Coffee sounds great," I said, which was true.

"Help yourself," Darryl said. "I won't be two minutes."

There were two ways to interpret that sentence. I chose the more charitable, in an effort to be in sync with the season, smiled at the three guests, who were watching me with wary eyes and non-committal faces, and let myself into Darryl's office, closing the door gently behind me.

And as it turned out, the charitable interpretation was accurate. I'd barely poured and whitened the liquid I'd found in the Mr. Coffee precariously perched on the edge of a dresser groaning under enough paper to reforest Boston, when the door opened and Darryl was with me.

"Sorry about that," he said, sweeping a stack of files off a chair and nodding me to it. "Have a seat and let me give you the facts."

The facts were more or less the same as they'd been in July, when the Shelter had done its big mid-summer fund raiser: twenty beds, a family unit, showers and laundry facilities available; breakfast and dinner served; no day-time accommodations. The Shelter had received more than seven thousand guests during the year, a disturbing number of them women and children.

"We've also been doing outreach," Darryl said, lounging behind his overloaded workspace, a chipped coffee mug bearing a huge yellow sunflower cradled in his hands. "The prevention program we instituted at the beginning of the year is, I think, doing a great deal of good."

He told me about the prevention program: A scheme whereby an "at-risk" person in low funds could pick up a free goody bag of food, soap, toothpaste, and laundry detergent at the Shelter, which allowed them to focus all of their income on paying the rent.

"Participation is limited to once every thirty days at the moment," Darryl said. "We're actively pursuing funds– Denise is working on a grant application right now–so we'll be able to do more with that."

"We're also looking at expanding the physical plant over the next eighteen months," Darryl said. "We've been talking to the town, and looking for funding. We've got plenty of knowledgeable volunteer labor already on-board, but we've got to cover the costs of materials . . ."

There was a little more. I made notes, asked a couple

questions, and Darryl put his empty mug on top of a pile of burgeoning file folders and gave me a smile.

"Anything else?"

I paused on the edge of shaking my head, recalling the intent faces, the taut bodies and intense hands . . .

"What was going on outside when I came in?" I asked.

Darryl blinked, and hesitated. I could almost see the wheels turning in that determined head of his, and wondered whether he was going to brush me off—gracefully, of course—

"Well," he said, and gave me another smile, this one shaded toward conspiratorial. "Off the record?"

"OK," I agreed, and slipped my pen and pad away with a smile of my own.

"Robert, Bev, and Larry are sort of ombudsmen; the guests voice concerns to them; if there seems to be a particular repeating area of concern, across a number of guests, then they bring the issue, whatever it may be, to staff." He shot me a glance to make sure I was still with the program. I nodded and smiled.

"Right, then. Apparently, there's some talk on the street that the Wimsy police may not be . . . trustworthy, let's say. Since the Shelter and its guests depend in large measure on the goodwill of the officers, this information was, as you might guess, pretty concerning."

"I'd guess so," I agreed. "Any idea what started the rumor?"

Darryl shrugged. "Couple things. There's drugs on the street now, which there didn't used to be. Since we serve people who are on the street, we hear about it. There's an assumption—among some of our more . . . sensitive . . . guests, you understand—that the police force could stop it, if they wanted to. These folks equate the fact that the problem continues with the police being on the take." He sighed, and shook his head.

"Also, I think we're seeing some over-reaction to the handling of that poor girl's death. The people the *Voice* interviewed seemed very certain that there was a cover-up; a crime that was being swept under the rug by the officers. That sort of feeds the general level of paranoia." He smiled again. "It'll blow over, I'm sure." He smiled again. "The 'news on the street' isn't always."

It's rare that one gets to see the consequences of one's actions quite so clearly. The coffee I'd just drunk was suddenly mixing badly with the gingerbread boy I'd eaten in place of lunch.

"It could just be that the police are mistaken," I said slowly. "They're only human, after all."

"That's right," Darryl said soothingly, his thoughts obviously already someplace else. He stood and held out his hand. "Thanks again for coming, Jen. I know I can count on you to get the story right."

20

I took the long way back to the *Voice*, in order to have time to examine my conscience. All very well and good to say that I only wrote down what people told me and allowed the paper's readers to form their own conclusions–but that didn't absolve me from any complicity in the conclusions they drew. I wasn't a neutral conduit; I was a human being, as fallible and as opinionated as they come. I *choose* who I talk to; I *choose* the quotes I pull out from my interview notes. I have the power to influence public opinion for or agin'– all, all by just by writing down what I've been told.

Spin is everything.

An ethical reporter tries to present all sides of a given issue equally, to give a balanced presentation on which readers can then base their conclusions. A reporter who takes sides–a reporter who manipulates the reader–who lets her own convictions shape the story . . .

That person is no reporter at all, and ought, in fairness to the readers she has misinformed and misled, put down her Bic and her pad and never report again.

And with those happy thoughts revolving in my brain, I turned into the *Voice*'s front door, and plodded up the stairs to the newsroom.

*

In contrast to my morning sojourn, the place was packed. Features was vibrating with the clatter of computer keys. Jack-the-Jock was at his desk, sorting through a pile of photos. I mooched on past without waving, still deep in my funk.

"Hey! Jen!" Jack yelled. I stopped, backed up two steps and looked at him, eyebrows up.

He grinned and raised a hand, waggling his fingers at me. "Hi there, Jen. Good to see you."

"Hey, Jack," I said, forcing a smile, and moved on.

Bill Jacques looked at me over the top of his glasses. Frowning, he stopped typing, raised a hand and took them off.

"Ms. Pierce. Are you quite well?"

I bit my lip, thought about passing by–then stepped up to the half-wall and leaned my purple parka clad elbows on the back of his computer. He might fire my ass, but the truth of the matter was that Bill Jacques was the expert on hand. If I really wanted to know what I thought I wanted to know, he was the man to ask.

"Bill," I swallowed around a gingerbread-boy-sized lump in my throat and forced myself to meet his eyes. "I– what do you do, if you've . . . misreported something?"

He crossed his arms over his chest, glasses dangling from his right hand, and pressed his lips together thoughtfully. Stomach clenched, I waited.

"Well," he said eventually. "What you do is, you fix it. Run a correction; run a retraction. Patch it up as best you're able." He considered me. "Anything I should know?"

"I'm not sure," I said slowly. "It's . . . complex . . . . To the point that I don't think a correction'll cover it."

"Well," he said again, and turned his head slightly, sending a glance toward Carly's empty desk before giving me his whole attention once more.

"What you do in the case of . . . complexity . . . is arrange a time for your editor to buy you a beer, so the two of you can sort it out in more convivial surroundings."

I considered him, my mood lightening somewhat. Bill nodded, uncrossed his arms and put his glasses back on.

"Because," he said, reaching for the keyboard, "as we all know, confession is good for the soul. And beer is just good."

I felt my lips twitch. "Hard to argue with that logic. Lunch tomorrow?"

"I have a luncheon appointment tomorrow, I'm afraid. How about tomorrow evening, at the Chez? Peggy's on, and we'll have the back table to ourselves while she sings for her supper."

"Deal," I said, and pushed away from the wall, walking back to hang up my coat with significantly less gloom in my heart.

*

Three o'clock. Milt was at his desk, typing briefs, for a wonder. I was going over the homeless shelter story for the third time, weighing every sentence for neutrality, making damn sure that I had only reported the facts, and that no inkling of my own feelings about the shelter had leaked onto the page. Dayside was busy, judging from the murmur of voices, and patter of keys. Into this scene of homey productivity came Jerry–or maybe it was John–Talbot, nattily attired in a white-and-red reindeer sweater and wool dress slacks.

"Attention everyone!" He yelled, his voice ringing off the walls, and rattling the cheap acoustic ceiling tiles in their metal frames. "I have an announcement to make!"

Silence grew slowly, but Jerry-or-John seemed patient, for once. The clatter of keys stopped first, then the mutter of voices as phones were hastily cradled, and conversations between coworkers were cut off in mid-word. Eventually, the room was eerily quiet, except for a sudden squawk out of the scanner. Bill Jacques reached up and turned it off.

"Thank you," said the Twin, and spun slowly on his heel, like he was taking a head count. When he got back to where he started, he raised his voice again.

"There will be a staff meeting today at five o'clock, in the upstairs conference room. This is not optional. All staff are required to attend. If you have an appointment at five o'clock, I suggest you cancel it now." He spun again, and pointed. At me.

"You," he said. "Call the staffers who aren't here and tell them to get themselves in here for the meeting."

Two desks in front of me, Milt sniggered, while I just sat there, too outraged to even gasp.

"Well?" asked the Twin. "Nothing to say, *Miss* Pierce?"

I wondered briefly if the guy who had commented on the banality of evil and the guy who had coined the phrase, "Payback is hell," had been roomies in college. I drew a long, careful breath and managed to produce a calm, "I'll get right to that, Mr. Talbot."

The Twin smirked, and swept out. I took another deep breath, and met Bill Jacques' eyes. He winked at me. Over in Dayside, computer keys began to clack again, raggedly.

"They're going to fire all of us at once," Milt caroled from first desk. "It's gonna be a friggin' blood bath. We'll all be out on the street at Christmas time—no food for baby, no fuel for fire—"

Bill turned his head.

"Shut up."

I would have been huddling under my desk in terror if Bill had spoken to me with anything approaching that distant iciness. However, Milt is not what you'd call sensitive to nuance.

"After all," he said, in defiance of orders; "none of us are employable, or why would we be working *here*, for Chrissakes? I tell you, it's going to be—"

"I said *shut up!*" That was a roar. Over in Dayside, the clatter of computer keys cut off, then deliberately resumed. Bill lowered his voice, but that somehow increased the vehemence.

"If I hear," he told Milt, "one more *stupid* word out of you, or another rumor of the sort you've just been spouting, you won't have to wait for that meeting, because *I'll* fire you on the spot! Are you straight on that?"

Milt gulped. "Sure, Bill."

"Fine," our editor bit out, and visibly took a breath. "Are you going to finish with those briefs any time soon, Mister Vane?"

"Comin' right up," Milt muttered, and hunched over his keyboard, while I picked up the phone.

I called over to paste-up first, to make sure they'd gotten the word.

"Oh, we got it," Brenda said direfully. "Nothing like setting things up in advance."

"Hey," I said, "they told us whole *hours* ahead."

"There's that," she acknowledged. "I'd love to chat, Jen, but I've got some calls to make—and, hey, thanks for calling over. 'Preciate the thought."

"No problem," I said, truthfully. "Later."

I hit the disconnect and dialed Sue Danforth's number.

" 'Lo! Danforth rez-i-dence," the young voice told me importantly.

"Hi, Molly, it's Jen from the paper. Can I talk to your mom?"

"Hold on," Molly told me and put the phone down with a clatter and a clank that did nothing to obscure the shouted, "Mo-om! Jen from the paper!"

There was some more clattering, then Sue, sounding breathless.

"Hi, Jen. What's up?"

"Command performance at five o'clock in the upstairs conference room. All staff required to attend."

I heard Sue draw a breath, and I waited interestedly, wondering if I was about to hear something uncharitable. But all she said was, "I'll drop Molly at my sister's early and be in. Thanks for calling."

"No problem—see you soon." We hung up.

I got Dan Skat on the car phone and passed the happy news; and left a message on Carly's machine. Having dispensed with the numbers I knew by heart, I pulled my Rolodex forward and was flicking through the cards, when I felt a presence nearby. I looked up, and wasn't as surprised as I should've been to find Serena Jefferson leaning her elbows on the half-wall behind my computer. Today's suit was rough woven azure wool, worn over an ivory silk turtleneck.

"Ms. Pierce, I'm glad I found you in," she said, when she saw she had my attention. "I've been wanting to tell you that you're an asset to this company."

I blinked. "An—asset?" I repeated, brilliantly.

Serena Jefferson smiled, and this one almost did reach her eyes. "Sorry. I'm so used to speaking in terms of assets and liabilities, professionally, that it leaks over into my social interactions. What I meant to say is that you're an ornament to this newspaper. Over the few days I've been in town, I've heard you referred to at the gas station, in the restaurant, and at the grocery store. They love you out there, Ms. Pierce—and they love what you're doing for this paper." She smiled again and straightened. "I'll let you get back to work; I know you're busy," she said. "But—do think about it, Ms. Pierce. You're a force in this town."

She moved away, past Milt and down to Bill Jacques' desk.

Great, I thought, stomach cramped anew; *some superstar, you are, Jen.*

Sighing, I went back to the Rolodex, and picked up the phone.

21

At four fifty-nine and three-quarters, all of the hastily gathered troops assembled in the *Voice*'s upstairs conference room. There were, of course, far more staff than chairs, so most of us were leaning against the walls, sitting on window sills or, in the case of Chance Maurand, standing at attention just inside the door.

The Twins, predictably, hadn't managed to get in yet. Neither had Carly, which worried me more. Sandwiched between Sue Danforth and Jack-the-Jock, I was furiously trying to dredge up the name of the guy she'd brought to the Christmas party out of my memory—Evan hadn't it been? Evan, Evan, *what?*—when there was a hurried clatter outside the door.

Those who had been leaning bonelessly tensed, and all faces turned toward the door.

Carly stopped on the threshold, coat unzipped and hair wind-snarled. She raised her hands, showing empty palms and gave a deep sigh.

"Oh, good; they're not here yet."

The room visibly relaxed and she squeezed in, edging her way back until she stood next to Jack-the-Jock.

"Jen—" She leaned across Jack and touched my arm. "Thanks for leaving the message on my machine. I was out Christmas shopping."

I nodded. "No problem," I told her. "I did the same for everybody."

Carly tipped her head, and sent a questioning glance into Jack's face as she eased back.

"That's right," Jack said. "Mr. Talbot decided that Jen looked like the newsroom secretary."

"We don't have a newsroom secretary," Carly muttered,

wriggling out of her coat, an exercise which seemed to interest Jack considerably. "Which Misters Talbot oughta darn well know."

"I guess firing Sheila wasn't all that memorable," Jack said.

"Just another game of kick the locals to them." Carly snarked. She looked rapidly around, coat in hand, then dropped it at her feet. "Has to be cleaned anyway," she muttered.

There was another movement at the door, this one considerably more subtle than Carly's entrance, and Serena Jackson stood on the threshold. She nodded, professionally pleasant, to the group as a whole, took a step forward, and checked. I was watching closely, so I saw her frown when her eyes fell on the vacant chairs around the conference table. By the time she looked up and around the room again, it was gone.

"We'll be just another moment," she said, her voice smooth and courteous. "Thank you for your patience–and your promptness."

She turned on her heel and was gone, walking lightly in her two hundred dollar heels.

On my left, Sue Danforth checked her watch and sighed. "If I'd known the meeting was going to start late, I wouldn't have rushed Molly out of the house without her blanket."

"Doesn't your sister have blankets?" I asked, and Sue smiled her tired smile.

"She does, but Molly has a *special* blanket–it's the grubbiest thing you've ever seen. She takes it with her everywhere. And I do *mean* everywhere. I just hope she gets over it before she goes to kindergarten."

"Don't count on it." Carly was leaning across Jack again, steadying herself with one hand on his arm. "My brother *still* has his security blanket! Twenty-two years old–it's just sad. His girlfriend even tried–"

Voices outside the conference room door. Carly

prudently pulled back without telling us what her brother's girlfriend had tried with regard to the security blanket problem—and the Talbot Twins strolled into the room, followed by Serena Jefferson.

The Twins took the seats to the immediate right and left, settling their papers—leaving the head of the table to Serena Jefferson, which was . . . interesting. It wasn't like The Twins to give up the power chair.

Serena Jefferson folded her hands on the table and looked around the room, making eye contact, her expression pleasantly noncommittal.

"Thank you once again for your promptness and your patience. We won't keep you long; I know you all have calls to make and people to see." She glanced to her right. "Mr. Talbot?"

John-or-Jerry nodded and cleared his throat. "As Ms. Jefferson says, we know you're busy, so we'll cut right to the chase, and let you get back to business." He glanced across at his brother.

"Right." He rustled his papers like he was actually looking for something, but he wasn't fooling anybody in the room with that dodge.

"The bottom line," he told his papers, "is that my brother and I have sold this newspaper to the Franklin Syndicate. The audit's been done and the paperwork has been signed. The Syndicate will take over operations on January 15. Any questions?" He lifted his head and glared around the room, daring anybody to ask.

Bill Jacques raised his hand. The Talbot glare grew icier, but Serena Jefferson inclined her head courteously. "Mr. Jacques?"

"Will you be coming aboard as managing editor, ma'am?"

"Ah." She smiled and shook her head. "I'm afraid I'm only a number-cruncher, Mr. Jacques. My official title is vice president in charge of acquisitions. The Syndicate believes in promoting from within. In general, when we acquire a property—and you'll understand that this is only a general outline, because every property is different—in general we'll bring in an editor from another Franklin paper for a few months. That editor will oversee the transition. They will also make staffing recommendations to Corporate. We make every effort to retain the staff already in place." She smiled again. "Does that answer your question?"

"Yes, ma'am," Bill said, in his blandest voice. "Thank you."

"Thank *you*." She looked around the room. "Any other questions? Ms. Pierce?"

All eyes turned my way, and for once in my life, I didn't have any— No, wait. I did have a question, after all.

"Will the schedule remain the same?"

She tipped her head, frowning slightly, then her face cleared. "Three days a week, you mean? For the time being, yes. After Corporate has evaluated the recommendations of the visiting editor, we'll have a clearer picture there." She paused, as if debating with herself, then inclined her head slightly.

"Franklin Syndicate has grown papers into dailies, when conditions warranted. We believe in community newspapers. Community newspapers are our base. We understand them and the factors that affect them very well."

Fair enough, though it came with a good helping of corp-speak worthy of a VP of acquisitions. After all, it had to be part of Serena Jefferson's job to soothe anxious employees and keep the Syndicate's acquisition in one piece until it decided how best to handle it.

"Thank you," I said, and she nodded, sending another glance around the room.

"Anything else?"

Nobody stepped forward. The Twins pushed back from the table and stood like the same puppeteer was pulling their strings.

"That's it, then," the one on the left said.

"Everybody can go back to work," the one the right added.

Serena Jefferson rose slowly. "If anyone thinks of something they'd like to ask—if you have any concerns whatsoever—I'll be here the rest of the week. Mr. Talbot has kindly let me use his office. You can find me there. Thank you all for coming."

She turned and left the room, flanked by The Twins. None of them looked back.

Which was just as well.

My co-workers stood silent. "Pole-axed" was the word that leapt to mind, granting that I wasn't feeling all that steady, myself. No one said anything, which was a measure of the depth of their shock.

Next to me, I felt Jack-the-Jock take a breath.

"I think that calls for a beer," he said, his voice overloud. "Who wants to join me?"

22

It was a pretty evening–cold, but not excessively so, and perfectly windless. The sort of evening that cleared the mind and braced the senses, if my grandfather was to be believed. I paused on the walk outside the *Voice*'s offices, took a deep breath, and sighed it out in a puff of frost.

Since going out for a beer and listening to endless interpretations of what had been said didn't much appeal to me; I'd gone down to my desk, finished up the Shelter story and sent it over to Bill Jacques, who apparently had no taste for beer this evening, either. Then I stuck around and entered some briefs while Sue went over to the cop shop to pick up the log–Milt having, predictably enough, opted for beer. I finally left the newsroom at six-thirty.

Not too bad for a shift that was supposed to have ended at five, but still a little too early to drive out to Fox's place– and no sense going back home, only to have to turn around and go back across town. Shaking my head, I walked away from Main Street, jolly in its holiday decorations, and across the parking lot.

In summer, with the trees in leaf, you can look down from the end of the parking lot and barely know the Smoke is there, though, if the day's quiet, you might hear the whisper of water a few feet below your toes.

In winter, with the trees asleep and only naked branches to bracket the view, you can see the river easy enough– in daylight. Six-thirty of a December evening in Central Maine, it's pitch dark, of course, and the only thing you can make out of the river is the glitter of a parking lot light against the ice. Just a little snow over the ice, but that hadn't stopped the snowmobilers. I could see sled tracks, black stripes on the gray surface.

Well, at least the ice was solid.

Tentatively, I let myself consider the news of the hour.

The Twins having sold the *Voice*–that should have been good news, and for all concerned. A clean break–that was the best, really, for The Twins and for the *Voice*.

But.

The Franklin Syndicate owned hundreds of small papers across the country. The Syndicate had a bottom line, so the scuttlebutt went, and those papers that didn't pull their weight–were closed.

It was hard–damn' hard–to see how a three-day-a-week paper out of Wimsy, Maine, was going to be able to toe the bottom line. A newspaper runs on advertising, and advertising income in Wimsy was thin on the ground. I didn't have access to the operating budget, but it was painfully clear every time I went through the paper that the ad line was lower and lower. No wonder The Twins had wanted to sell.

And the Franklin Syndicate, if it actually wanted to preserve a newspaper presence in Wimsy, was going to have to cut costs, which meant letting people go. Which meant that this was one of those rare, precious times that Milt Vane was actually right–a bloodbath was in the offing.

Well. I shook my head at the river, and turned back toward the lot. Maybe a reporter who was an "asset" to the *Voice* didn't have anything to–

Somebody grabbed my arm.

I yanked back, a yell throttling in my throat.

"No, hey, hey, s'okay, OK?" The voice was blurry, the grip on my arm none too firm. "C'mon, hey, it's only me–Jimmy."

"Let me go," I said, and heard my voice quaver.

"Sure, no problem." He released me and stepped back, which put him in the puddle of light from the street lamp. I smelled beer. A lot of beer.

Jimmy Danforth is a small man, wiry rather than

muscled. He was wearing a denim jacket buttoned to his chin, collar turned up around his ears, jeans and a pair of sneakers. *Not* seasonally correct clothing, by any means. He fumbled in his pocket, produced a rumpled soft-pack and shook a cigarette loose.

"Smoke?"

"No, thanks." I'd recovered my balance now. Jimmy was drunk, but not pissed-at-the-whole-fucking-world-drunk. Not yet. Now, he was feeling sociable.

"Look, Jimmy, I've got an appoint–"

He snapped a cheap lighter, the flare underlit his face for a second–black brows, shadowed black eyes, black beard merging with straggling black hair.

"It's OK," he slurred. "Only wanted to say–you lookin' for a story? Maybe got something to do with that girl got killed."

I went still. "Yes," I said cautiously.

He blew smoke in a long sigh and tucked the lighter away. "I got a story for you. Big story, just for you. I'll show you– everythin'. You gotta pay for it, though."

I considered him. "Why not just tell the cops, if you know something about the girl who got killed?"

Jimmy laughed, then coughed noisily, turned his head and spat. "Sure, sure. I go up to the cops and tell 'em somethin' innerestin' and the cops say, 'Jimmy, go home and sleep it off'." He spat again. " 'Sides, the French cop's dirty. Can't trust 'im."

I frowned. The "French cop" had to be Ken Aube, but– "Dirty?" I repeated.

"Yeah, yeah. Everybody knows." He took a drag on his cigarette.

"Knows what?" I asked, when he didn't say anything else.

"Smokes," Jimmy said. "But that ain't what's innerestin'. Gotta show it, else you won't believe me. 'Sides, you need to take pictures, right? Back it up?"

"That's right," I said, deciding to go with the flow for

the moment. "When?"

"Tomorrow? Give you time to get the money. You gotta pay for this, Jen. No freebies, right?"

"Right. How much?" I asked, thinking of the ten dollar bill in my wallet.

"Fifty dollars."

"*Fifty*–!"

He held up a hand. "Hey, it's Christmas. An' look–if it ain't that innerestin', you don't have to pay. Deal?"

Well, that was certainly fair enough, especially considering that this farce was undoubtedly being directed by the beer and the "interesting stuff" was probably no more than imagination.

"Sure, it's a deal."

Jimmy grinned. "Good. You meet me right here tomorrow, four o'clock sharp, and I'll show you."

I blinked, looked around at the December parking lot, and back to Jimmy. "Here?"

"Nah, nah, it ain't here. You meet me here. Then we'll go on down to the landing together."

I sighed. "What stops me from going down to the landing right now without you and saving myself fifty dollars?"

Jimmy took a drag on his cigarette. "Won't be there 'til tomorrow. And you need me to show you where."

It sounded like Jimmy had been seeing too many B-grade videos. I swallowed a serious inclination to laugh. "OK, Jimmy. Tomorrow at four, here, and we'll go down to the old ferry landing. I'll see you." I started to walk past.

He grabbed my arm. His grip this time was harder. I stopped.

"Bring cash," he hissed in my ear and I nodded, but he didn't let me go, not quite then.

Instead, he looked over his shoulder again, then whispered, "She recognized him. Now she's dead."

He did let me go then, and I spun, heart thumping hard. "Hey–"

But Jimmy was running across the parking lot toward Main Street.

*

I pulled in next to the green four-by-four and killed the Camaro's engine. The dashboard clock read seven-ten.

At the front door I used the knocker and waited. In fact, I waited so long, I was reaching for the knocker again when the door opened and Fox blinked at me through gold-rimmed glasses.

"Jennifer?" He pulled the glasses off, flicked them shut and stowed them in his breast pocket. "Sorry–I forget I have them on until the far world goes all blurry . . . I left a message on your– You haven't been home."

I shook my head. "The Twins called a five o'clock staff meeting." I swallowed, feeling abruptly and absurdly bereft. "I can leave, if you're busy."

"I'm not that busy," Fox said, and stepped back, opening the door wide. "But I'm sorry that you've made the trip for nothing."

Two steps into the hall, I stopped. "Grant McElroy didn't have Carl install a new hard drive?"

Fox shut the door and engaged the lock with a snap, then turned to look at me, one eyebrow up.

"He had Carl install the new drive. It's just that he wanted the old one back."

I stared at him. "Why?"

"A reasonable question. Carl seems to feel it's on the order of demanding the worn parts back from one's mechanic and is suitably offended. May I take your coat?"

I unzipped the parka and let him take it off my shoulders and hang it up while I stared at nothing in particular and tried to come up with a logical reason for Grant McElroy, inn owner and computer novice, to want a fried and useless hard drive returned to him.

"Coffee?" asked Fox, jogging me out of my funk. I shook my head and focused on him.

"Fox, look, if you're busy, I can just– "

"We're past that part," he said, taking me gently by the arm and steering me down the hall and then right, into the kitchen. "We're now at the top of the next page, where I ask you to fill me in on what you've discovered so far, and discuss your feelings vis-à-vis letting the whole thing drop versus going for the gold. Coffee?"

"I never did hear about Mr. Wiley," I said, planting my feet. Fox raised an eyebrow.

"Mr. Wiley is another satisfied customer. He will shortly receive a monumental bill, which should nicely reinforce my threat to be unavailable to him at any price the next time he mucks up my code."

"Poor Mr. Wiley."

"Mr. Wiley has purchased everything he is being billed for," Fox told me. "*Do* you want coffee, Jennifer? Or would you prefer a glass of wine?"

"Coffee would be great," I said automatically. He nodded and moved toward the counter.

"Now that we've laid Mr. Wylie to rest, you may have the floor."

I sighed and wandered over to the table, leaning both palms on the back of a wooden ladder chair and watching Fox dump a cupful of old brew down the sink and rinse the coffeepot.

"I don't have any facts," I said, thinking of Jimmy Danforth. "Like I said this morning. What I've got is the conviction of every single person who knew her that Lisa wouldn't have shot herself and a lot of stuff that's funny, but not necessarily fatal."

"Like the gentleman who took a pet upon finding a body in his room and left without paying his bill."

"Like him. Like the fact that the Mill's hard drive melted *now*. Like Grant McElroy wanting the bad drive back.

Like Ken Aube not being on the door when Dan snuck up to get a picture. Like Lisa not leaving a note. Like Jimmy–"

I caught myself almost too late. I hadn't meant to tell Fox about Jimmy Danforth. Intuition suggested that Fox would take a very dim view of Jimmy Danforth, to say nothing of fifty dollar cash transactions based on "interesting things" supposedly situated at the end of an isolated road in the dim afternoon of winter. Besides, I told myself not quite truthfully, I hadn't made up my mind whether I was going to go.

"Not to mention," I babbled, to cover my misstep, "the question of where Grant McElroy's computer got a virus in the first place. The help was supposed to be backing the drive up on floppies, but they weren't, so unless somebody brought a game to work . . ." I stopped, suddenly recalling a disk–a disk jiggling up and down, up and down, held between Ken Aube's thumb and forefinger . . .

Circumstance, Jen, my sensible side whispered, but sensible had long since left the building.

"Ken Aube had a disk with a virus on it," I told Fox's back. "Ken Aube was the first cop on the scene." *Ken Aube killed Lisa,* my not-so-sensible side whispered, but that was beyond jumping to conclusions. Grant McElroy might have killed Lisa–or the mystery man with the guns in his luggage. Ken might just be part of the cover-up–if there was a cover-up. If Lisa hadn't, against all odds, committed suicide. If, if, if–*the French cop's dirty,* Jimmy whispered in my backbrain, and I shivered.

Fox flicked the switch on the coffeemaker and turned to face me, one hip against the counter and his arms crossed over his chest.

"You think the police are covering up."

"At the very least, I think Ken Aube is covering up–something." *And the rest are letting him . . .*

He nodded, coffeemaker burbling loudly behind him. "That does make life simpler."

I stared. "How?"

"Well, we don't necessarily need Mr. McElroy's fried drive. If there's a cover-up at the police level, we might be able to find some interesting tidbits in the police department's network."

"In the—" I looked at him, but he seemed just as calm and as grave as always. "You're willing to hack the police station's network?"

"In a good cause."

I gripped the ladder back and glared. "You'll get caught."

Fox sighed sharply and shifted against the counter. "Kathy used to say that," he observed, rather irritably, "but Kathy didn't know anything about computers. You know about computers—and you certainly know that I'm *not* going to get caught. Even if someone happens to notice me in the system, so what? I put the network together. I'm the pro. Why shouldn't I do a spot check to be sure everything's functioning as it should? If the police chief doesn't like it, he'll tell me, and that will be the end of the matter. But it's not a question of being *caught*. I haven't been caught yet." The coffeemaker gave one last burble and beeped.

Yet. I took a deep breath and said, with what I thought was really commendable calm: "I think you'd better tell me who you are."

Both eyebrows shot up. "The Hacker from the Black Lagoon."

I mustered another glare. "Thank you."

"You're quite welcome. The milk's in the fridge." He turned away to pull the basket out of the coffeemaker.

Back tight, I stalked over to the refrigerator and yanked the door open.

I got back to the table as Fox was settling the mugs. I put the milk carton down, pulled out a chair and sat. After a moment Fox sat, too.

"I can look around in the police computers if you think it will do you some good," he said, very quietly. "If you would rather I didn't, then I'll abide by your choice."

I looked at him: calm, his eyes straight, serious and absolutely steady. My call, and Fox would stand by it. I took a careful breath. "Thank you. I would prefer that you did not look around in the police network. Ken's covering something up, but it might not have one thing to do with Lisa's death."

"All right," he said, pouring milk into his mug. He handed the carton to me and I poured in turn, relieved we had brushed past the trouble spot.

"Now," Fox said, stirring his coffee gently, "who's Jimmy?"

23

I sighed to myself and studiously stirred my coffee, eyes on the swirling beige surface.

Damn, I thought, and then: *Honestly, Jennifer, tell the man who Jimmy is and what he says he has. So he's not going to like the set up. You don't like the set up, either.* But I knew I was going to be at the parking lot tomorrow afternoon, fifty bucks from my savings account tucked inside the parka's pocket, on the off-chance Jimmy Danforth actually would show up–and actually knew something worth his price.

"Not," Fox prodded softly from across the table, "like Harry?"

I sighed again, audibly, and put my spoon aside. "Harry's a special case," I said and looked up, surprising wariness in his eyes for the second time in twenty-four hours.

"Jimmy Danforth," I said briskly, to take my mind off the sudden squeezing around my heart, "is one of the town's bad boys. He was married to Sue Danforth before she got tired of getting smacked around and threw him out. So now Jimmy's on the town. He used to drive a log rig, but he lost his license. Now he works odd jobs, in the woods or out, when he works at all. Mostly, he gets drunk, picks fights, steals cigarettes, spends a couple nights in jail every month and in general raises minor but aggravating hell. OK?"

Fox sipped coffee. "You have the oddest friends," he commented. "Where does Jimmy figure into Lisa's death, do you think?"

"I don't think he does." I had recourse to my mug, then set it precisely on the table, curling my hands around it as I met Fox's eyes.

"Jimmy says he has something 'interesting' to show

me down at the old ferry landing, and suggests, but doesn't say outright, that it could tie in with 'the girl who died'–his quotes. I'm supposed to pick him up tomorrow afternoon, with cash in hand. Jimmy promises to show Mr. Grant something that will knock his socks off, or my money cheerfully refunded."

Fox frowned. "Fifty dollars?"

"You think that's too much?"

"That rather depends on what he knows, doesn't it?" he said, and I heard the shadow of what might be his mother's accent in his voice before he sighed. "Is he likely to know anything?"

I'd been thinking about that one. Hard.

"It's possible. Jimmy gets all over town–and he's just the town drunk, so people sort of know he's around without specifically noticing if he's right next to them, if you see what I mean."

Fox nodded. "He's the Wimsy equivalent of the postman."

"Don't tell me you're an Agatha Christie fan."

" 'Fan' might be too strong. I have, however, sampled her work." He glanced down, apparently fascinated by the contents of his mug.

I drank my cooling coffee and waited, fairly certain that I knew what was coming.

Eventually, he looked up, face cautious, eyes intent.

"You're not going to thank me for meddling and I'm well aware that it's your story, your shift and your decision," he began. His voice was painfully level and I suddenly wondered about Kathy Foxwell. Fox was behaving like a man all too familiar with the dangers inherent in dealing with wrong-headed women.

"And has it occurred to me that this is not exactly a wise course of action?" I finished, to let him off the hook. "Yes, it has."

He sighed. "But."

"But, if I don't find out—if I don't do my damnedest to find out the truth—to *settle* the thing, once and for all, then . . . then there's damage done that won't go away. That will fester and . . ." I stopped, took a breath and looked close into his eyes. "I've done— I might have done—something that's actually and truly bad, on a cosmic scale of bad."

Fox raised an eyebrow and settled back in his chair, waiting for whatever I felt like telling him.

"I—a reporter has to be careful to give equal time to all sides of a story, when there are sides. If you give more ink to one side or another, if you only pull quotes that make one side look stupid, or obstructive, or . . . You can spin the story, make the readers believe what you want them to believe." I took a breath. Fox's eyes never wavered.

"So, I gave ink to all those people who don't believe— who can't believe—that Lisa shot herself. So much ink and so much attention that it looks like the police *have* to be covering something up. It happens that *I* believe Lisa couldn't have shot herself, but I had no business letting that color my reporting. And now there's damage done.

"In a small town, people know who to trust, and how far to trust them. You trust the cops, even if you don't like them, even if some of them steal and some of them brawl and some of them are tougher than they strictly need to be. The cops teach kids to say no to drugs and they tell you when your back left brake light's out. You trust the cops to protect you— life, limb and property. And they do that, mostly. Here, they do. Some towns have bad cops. On the whole, Wimsy has good cops." *Except Jimmy had said that everybody knew Ken Aube was "dirty." Was that true or was that the beer talking?*

"And now, the word is going around that the cops are covering something up." Fox's voice was very quiet.

I nodded. "Because of me. Because of how I chose to report the story. If I was wrong—" I shook my head. "I've got to know if I was wrong, and if I was, I need to, to—"

"Tell the truth and shame the devil."

I smiled again, suddenly very, very tired. "Like that."

"All right." He paused. "Will you at least be taking a gun with you tomorrow?"

I blinked. "I don't have a gun."

"I do," said Fox.

*

It was snub-nosed, black and business-like. Fox handled it like he knew what he was doing, which he probably did. After all, this was the gun he had chosen to kill the man who had murdered his wife.

I licked my lips. I'd seen guns before. My uncle the cop had carried a gun. But his had been chastely snapped into its holster, quiescent and mannerly within its bond of peace. This gun was–a wild card; naked, gleaming–deadly.

"Do you–" I cleared my throat. "Do you have a license for that?"

Fox closed his eyes briefly. "The woman wants a legal gun," he said softly. He looked at me.

"Jennifer, the Constitution guarantees citizens of the United States of America the right to bear arms. By an amendment to that same document, persons of your gender are recognized as citizens of the United States of America. Therefore, this is a legal gun. All right?"

I glared at him. "How did you live to grow up?"

"I run fast and I'm smart," Fox said. "On balance, I'd say it was running fast far more than smart. Now, pay attention."

He picked up the gun, muzzle pointed modestly toward the floor. "Tell me, what do you know about guns?"

I sighed. "I know not to touch them."

"A poor beginning, but one from which great strides may easily be made. Hold out your hand."

I did, trying not to look as squeamish as I felt. Fox slid the gun into my palm–the grip was still warm from his hand–

and shaped my fingers around it.

"Like so. Pointed at the floor, please. It's not loaded, but why take chances? Now, just hold it for a moment or two." He slanted a bright cobalt glance into my face. "It won't bite you. It's a machine—like a computer or a car. It can only act when you give it leave, and then only to your specifications."

I nodded, then looked down at my hand, wrapped around the gun. It was heavy, but not as heavy as I'd imagined it would be.

"This is a Smith and Wesson snub-nose revolver," Fox said, quietly instructive. "It holds five bullets. In a moment, I'll show you how to load it."

I licked my lips and looked up to his face, which was composed as always, no hint of humor at the corner of the mouth, no spark of mischief in the eyes.

"Fox," I said and my voice was creaky. I cleared my throat and tried again. "Fox, I don't think this is a good idea."

He sighed. "Frankly, I don't think it's a good idea either, but it doesn't appear that my chances of talking you out of it are very high."

"I meant—the gun. I don't think the gun's a good idea. I'm just going to go meet Jimmy. He's going to show me his big secret, which is probably something the beer whispered in his ear, and I'll go back to work. I don't need a gun for that. I need a notebook, a Bic, and five ten dollar bills."

He was silent for a beat of three, then said, very quietly. "Jennifer, someone shot Lisa and now Lisa is dead. There is a short list of people who definitely did not do it, but unless you can tell me Jimmy is on that list, I think we have to assume that he could have done it." He cocked his head. "Is he on the 'Definitely Not' list?"

I opened my mouth. Closed it and shook my head.

"All right," said Fox. "That being the case, to go with him alone to a destination of his choosing is foolhardy. To meet with him alone and unarmed is suicidal." His mouth was grim. "Don't suicide on me, Jennifer."

I looked at his face, so deadly earnest, then back at the gun, so potentially deadly.

"OK," I said, and sighed. "Teach me to load it."

24

I finished up the last brief in the pile at three-fifty, sent the whole batch over to Carly's queue, and shut down my computer. I walked to the back, signed out the spare camera, shrugged into my parka and headed out.

Bill Jacques looked up over his glasses as I paused by his station.

"Ms. Pierce. Going out for a spot of Christmas shopping?"

"Nothing so pleasant." I showed him the camera. "Jimmy Danforth wants to show me something at the old ferry landing. Chances are I'm going to be stood up, but even if not, I shouldn't be long."

He nodded. "Is our meeting still on for this evening?"

"Sure thing. The Chez, at–seven?"

"Peggy's on at eight. Let's split the difference and say– seven-thirty?"

"Done," I told him, turned–

"How long did you say you'd be out?" Bill asked.

I threw him a grin over my shoulder. "If I'm not back by five o'clock, call the cops."

He smiled, and glanced back down at his screen.

*

It was straight up four o'clock by the dashboard clock when I started up the Camaro and swung around to the back lot. For a wonder, Jimmy was waiting for me, hunched against the light pole nearest the river, a Big Apple paper coffee cup in one hand, and a cigarette in the other. I brought the Camaro in next to him, reached over and popped the door. He took a deep drag on the cigarette and dropped it, grinding it under his heel before he slid in.

"You brought the money, right?" he asked. "And the camera?"

"Are you still sure you've got something wonderful to show me?" I countered.

Jimmy sent me a darkling glance, and reached up to pulled the seat belt across. He wasn't looking all that good this afternoon; his face was greyish, and there were hard lines between his eyebrows. "You think I was so drunk I just made it all up?" he asked, and snapped the belt home. "Ferry landing," he said, like he was directing a cabbie, and took a drink from his cup.

Sighing to myself, I eased the car out of the lot and down Main Street.

*

At four-fifteen, I pulled across furrows of snow covered frozen mud at the end of the Point Road, and made as wide a turn as circumstances allowed, until the Camaro's nose was pointing back up the hill, toward home. Then I killed the engine and unsnapped the seat belt. The keys came out of the ignition and went into purple parka's breast pocket. I pressed the Velcro seal closed, and considered our immediate surroundings.

If I hadn't known that the Wimsy Snowskimmers Snowmobile Club used the parking lot as a semi-official gather-place, the runner-grooved snow and the overflowing trashcan beneath the single street light would've given me a hint. There were no signs of actual snowmobiles this afternoon, though.

Or anything else.

"This the place?" I asked Jimmy, who hadn't said a word since we'd gotten underway.

He sighed and turned his head to look at me.

"You got the money, Jen? I told you, this ain't a freebie."

I hesitated, but really, I'd come this far, it would to stupid to balk now. I pulled the folded bills out of my pocket and handed them over. He unfolded and fanned them, then shoved them into the pocket of his jeans. And I was betting that was the last I was going to see of my fifty bucks, whether or not Jimmy delivered.

"So," I said, sounding snappish in my own ears. "Where is this marvel?"

Jimmy grinned, and opened the door. "Right this way," he said, and headed off across the ridged and tricky surface, toward the path to the old ticket office.

I swore, grabbed the camera off the seat, and went after him.

Back in September, when I'd been doing my research for the article for *Maine Life*, I'd visited this very site and taken pictures of the vacant lot, the lone light pole, the river, bracketed by pretty autumnal trees. I'd even ventured a few steps down the overgrown trail toward the abandoned postal/telegraph/ticket office, but a glimpse of what was left of the building through the clinging vegetation convinced me that this was not a photograph that "our readership" would find the least bit quaint.

Winter had stripped the trees naked, and snow weighted the evergreen branches. Dusk wasn't too far in our future–I realized with a tingle that today was the Winter Solstice, the shortest day of the year. Jimmy's big surprise had better not be too far into the woods, or we'd be overtaken by the dark.

Jimmy paused by the big pine tree that camouflaged the trail head to glance over his shoulder. Assured that I was pursuing, albeit at a distance, he plunged into the dimness beyond the pine.

I came to the big pine–and stopped, looking at the snow-slicked trail with dismay.

I don't like this Jennifer, I told myself. *You should have listened to your better nature. Failing that, you should have listened to Fox.*

But I hadn't done either, and now the die was cast.

I took a deep breath and mentally did an inventory. In my right pocket was Fox's gun, loaded; in my left was a pad and a pen. The camera was slung over my shoulder by its strap. Yessir, I was ready for anything.

Despite which, I remained by the tree, as if my boots had frozen to the snow.

C'mon, Jen, you paid fifty bucks for this. Don't you want to see how it all turns out?

Well, yes. I was here for good and compelling reasons—reasons which still existed, though they had lost a little of their urgency in the chill immediacy of the moment. And to be perfectly honest, I wasn't all that crazy about being alone with Jimmy Danforth in the dark woods.

And, yes, I should've thought about that earlier.

I took another deep, bracing breath of icy air, and stepped away from the tree, setting my foot on the trail. There. I'd go see whatever-it-was, and come back. Piece of cake. I wasn't, I told myself, moving down the dim path, afraid of Jimmy Danforth.

The trail was twisty and convoluted, as if whoever had cut it had opted for less hacking and more walking. It was also slick, downright treacherous in spots, and littered with twigs, cones, pine needles, and acorns, among which I could see footprints that I assumed were Jimmy's. The further I got from the parking lot, the dimmer it became, and I wished I had remembered to bring a flashlight.

It was quiet on the trail. Far away up river, traveling easily on the icy air, I heard the throaty *zzzzzzZZET* of a two-stroke engine, winding out, and another one, just a little behind. Snowmobilers, I thought, joy-riding the Smoke. I wished I was with them—or anyplace else, actually, than where I was.

The old building was on my left. The path swung wide, into a dark and overgrown knot of bare branch and pine boughs, and dead-ended at a brown bush, its desiccated leaves clattering in the minor breeze.

I stumbled to a halt, staring around me, and gasped when a hand shot out of the noisy shadows and pulled me behind the bush.

"Quiet!" Jimmy Danforth hissed. "You think this is a game? Now, look." He pushed my shoulder, almost knocking me off my feet. When I got sorted out, I saw that we had an excellent view of what was left of the front wall of the old ticket office.

"Look at *what?*" I hissed back and Jimmy grunted.

"Give it a minute . . ."

I opened my mouth—and shut it. I had, after all, paid for this.

We stood, silent and motionless in our scanty hiding place, for considerably longer than a minute. My feet in their winter boots went from toasty to cold, and my ears were starting to burn in the small insistent breeze. The trees around us creaked and snapped, birds called. The snowmobiles were still riding the river, the sound of their engines closer—and suddenly very close indeed, as they came around the slight bend in the river, slowing, slowing . . .

Snow crunched and branches snapped as the machines turned off the ice and onto the snowy shore. I held my breath and drew in on myself, as if I could become invisible.

"Here we go," Jimmy whispered, sounding satisfied. "You better get that camera ready."

Right. I slid the strap off my shoulder, got the lens cap off, and held the camera in both hands, waiting, as the sounds of boots crunching through snow came nearer and nearer.

I took a deliberate breath, trying to still jangling nerves. *Honestly, Jen, it's probably a just couple of kids come down to take advantage of the privacy of the old building. You're letting Jimmy's cloak and dagger riff spook you.*

That was a comforting thought—for about thirty-five seconds.

Then the bushes across from our station parted and Ken Aube walked into the clearing, wearing snowmobiler's coveralls, his hands tucked into the pockets.

Followed by Grant McElroy, similarly attired.

". . . took the money," McElroy was saying.

I lowered the camera.

Ken turned. "I took the money, yeah. You and Alexander were running cigarettes–that's what you told me. Hell, why shouldn't I take the money? People been running cigarettes through Wimsy since I was a kid." I saw his shoulders lift and then fall–big, big breath, there.

"You're not running any cigarettes," it was said with bleak and absolute certainty.

"We did at first," Grant McElroy objected, his voice calm and businesslike. He unzipped the pockets of his suit, and pulled off his right glove. "But the percentage in cigarettes is 'way down, Ken. We weren't making any money to speak of, after your commission. We had to diversify."

"Diversify." Ken repeated, then, hard voiced. "What is it?"

"A little weed, a little coke; whatever Dwight's sources can get for him. Look– most of it goes on from here, if that's what's eating you. Only a fraction stays in Wimsy." He shoved the glove into his right pocket, his hand staying there.

I took a slow, careful breath. Beside me, Jimmy might've been an ice sculpture.

Grant McElroy shook his head. "The distributors are making their pickups tonight. You'll get your commission tomorrow, just like always."

Ken shook his head. "No," he said.

McElroy tipped his head, as if he hadn't quite heard, and repeated, "No? What's that–oh, I get it!" He laughed. "You want a bigger percentage, is that it? I'll have to talk it over with Dwight, but I think we can probably do something more for you. After all, it's Christmas."

"I meant," Ken said slowly, "no. I'm not taking any

more 'commissions', and I'm done 'looking the other way.' "

McElroy shook his head, chidingly. "I'd take a minute to think that over, Ken."

"I've thought it over," Ken said, unzipping his left breast pocket. He produced a folder and flipped it open. "You're under arrest for possession and intent to deal, and for the murder of Lisa Gagnon." His right hand came out of its pocket, holding a gun.

I reached out, carefully, and grabbed Jimmy's arm. He looked at me, eyes wide, and I jerked my head toward the parking lot. He nodded.

Blessedly, the bush didn't rattle as I eased by. It was closing in on dark, back here in the trees, and I went down the trail as quickly as I dared, keeping a sharp lookout and making sure I didn't step on any twigs. Despite my best care, my boots did crunch a little on the snow, but not enough to reach the two men in the clearing.

I hoped.

Halfway to the end of the trail I noticed that Jimmy wasn't with me.

Swearing under my breath, I swung back–and froze where I stood.

From the parking lot came the unmistakable sound of tires crushing snow. I held my breath, listening, but the car didn't continue back up the hill, as might someone who had blundered accidentally down to the dead-end.

I heard a car door close, quietly, and looked feverishly about me for a hiding place. No friendly bush was evident in the murk, but there was a fir tree just a few steps off the trail. I was behind it in two seconds flat, my right hand in the pocket of my parka, my fingers curled around the grip of Fox's gun.

Footsteps crunched up the path. I bit my lip and concentrated very hard on being invisible. More crunching, close now, and the beam of a flashlight illuminating the snowy path.

The footsteps stopped, the beam of light kissed my

footprints, and followed them off the trail. I eased the gun out of my pocket.

"Jennifer." His voice was soft and grave. "It's Fox."

I slipped the gun back into my pocket and stepped out onto the path.

"Put out the light," I whispered, and the beam flicked off as Fox came to my side.

"What are you doing here?" I hissed, while my backbrain tried to decide if I was furious or relieved.

He looked at me from the depths of his hood; I knew that because his head moved. It was far too dark to read his expression.

"I decided that I really didn't want to make a habit of allowing women I care about to endanger themselves while I'm not with them."

I blinked, and after a second or two remembered to close my mouth.

Behind us, a shot shattered the icy silence.

I gasped, and grabbed Fox's arm.

"Do you know anything about that?" he asked.

"Ken Aube–was arresting Grant McElroy," I started, and shook my head. "It's complicated."

"Then it will wait until we're someplace else," Fox decided. He took my hand and began walking back down the trail, toward the parking lot. Around us, the woods were once again absolutely silent; even the wind had died.

Half-a-dozen steps was all we went before the silence was shattered by rapid crunching footsteps.

"Jimmy," I said, turning–Fox squeezed my hand.

"This way, Jennifer. Jimmy can meet us in the parking lot."

He pulled me with him, moving quickly now, not quite a run, but certainly faster than was strictly prudent.

Behind us, footsteps skittered, slid; and then Jimmy's voice, perfectly audible over footsteps still crunching implacably onward, "Shit!"–followed by another shot, louder than the first.

Fox yanked me into a run, but the footsteps behind us were running, too, as whoever it was–Grant McElroy? Ken? One of the nameless distributors?–leapt into pursuit.

Fox slipped on the snow.

He twisted, and went down hard on his knees, dragging me with him.

I gasped on impact, bit my lip, scrambled up, slid–and steadied as an arm went 'round my waist.

The instant I was steady he let me go, and pushed me forward.

"Run."

There are times when even I know better than to argue.

I ran, and heard him crunching snow behind me, likewise, our pursuer. Closer now, I thought, and then tried to think of nothing but running, and keeping my–

For the third time, a shot.

I leapt forward, whipping around the sentinel pine at the end of the trail, and froze, waiting for Fox.

Who was face down on the trail about eight feet away from where I stood in scant cover. He wasn't moving.

Horror is a peculiar thing. I stood in the wounded silence, looking at the body of my friend, while an unknown marksman leisurely perused his options for wasting me, and felt no emotion, no fear–only a tremendously heightened awareness of my surroundings, of the cold on my face, the scent of the pine tree, the weight of the pistol in my pocket.

There came the sound of cautious footsteps across the brittle snow, and Grant McElroy stepped past Fox, his weapon ready, his eyes scanning the path.

Coolly, in no hurry whatsoever, I pulled the gun from my pocket, held it in both hands the way Fox had shown me, and swung out onto the path.

Grant McElroy's head snapped up; his gun rose–and I fired.

I missed, of course, and the gun kicked against my

hands like a jackhammer. I jumped in shock, and fired again as my feet skidded on the snow. Slipping, I slid and lost the gun, and there was blood, high on his right arm, black against the orange snowsuit, but the gun never faltered.

I got my feet under me and went to the left, trying to twist out of his sights, seeing a blue flicker in the corner of my eye–and suddenly Grant McElroy was flat on the snow and Fox was kicking the gun away, the flashlight held, reversed and ready, in his hand.

I climbed to my feet, and heard the siren, then, 'way up at the top of the hill.

"Are you all right?" I asked, very calmly.

Fox looked up and was at my side in two long strides, grabbing both my arms, hard.

"You're an idiot, do you know that?" he demanded, his voice was shaking.

"I'll take that as an affirmative," I said.

And burst into tears.

25

"So, Foxy," Peggy Neuman nestled her chin in her palm and gazed at him soulfully. "What was she supposed to do?"

Improbably, I was only a few minute's late for my date with Bill at the Chez, where we were all around the infamous Back Table: Fox, Peggy, Bill Jacques, and me. Fox and I had just finished narrating the events of the afternoon and it was now Q&A time.

"Run," Fox said succinctly. Bill Jacques laughed. Peggy shook her head.

"I thought you were dead," I pointed out for the third time since we'd been released from the police station on our own recognizance.

"All the more reason to run," Fox said, which made his three. "There is absolutely no documentation to support the theory that human sacrifice reanimates the dead."

I glared at him. "I suppose playing possum until the enemy comes close enough for you to hit him on the head is safety first?"

"Children!" Bill Jacques tapped his beer bottle with a quarter. "The court will rule." He raised a hand and looked at Peggy. She wiggled her eyebrows, mouth quirking.

"I see that Ms. Neuman and I are unanimous in our reading of this case." He pointed, first at Fox, then at me. "You're both idiots."

"Very well," Fox said, "if the court so rules . . ." He turned in his chair to face me.

"Jennifer, I was an idiot. Please forgive me." He held out a hand.

I slid my fingers around his and looked into quizzical

cobalt eyes. "Fox, I was an idiot. Please forgive me," I said, matching him solemn for solemn.

"You may kiss the bride," Bill said *sotto voce*. I started to glare at him over Fox's shoulder, then changed my mind and smiled.

"Thanks for calling the cops."

Bill sipped his beer. "Never let it be said that editorial fails in its duty to safeguard the reporters under its care." He straightened.

"Now," he said briskly, "some news you might not have heard. John Therriault tells me that Ken, Jimmy, and Grant McElroy are all recovering nicely, though Mr. McElroy has a fierce headache. Ken has resigned from the force, but is, in John's phrasing, 'cooperating.' And, in another part of the forest, Dwight Alexander has been picked up by the New Jersey State Police, who promise to send him back in a timely manner."

"Wow," I said. "That's quick—wait a minute. John told *you?*"

"Well, yes. I can hardly put Sue Danforth on the story, and I certainly can't assign it to you. Giving it to Milt is, as I think you'll agree, completely out of the question, which leaves—me."

"I'm sure Bill will do a fine job," Fox murmured. "You're in good hands, Jennifer."

"That's right, Jen," Peggy chimed in. "Bill was a hot dog reporter, back in the day. He's been telling me all about it."

"Not," Bill said placidly, pushing his chair back, "*all* about it." He stood. "Refills, anyone?"

Peggy handed him her empty glass. "The usual, please?"

"Certainly. Anyone else? David? Jennifer?"

I shook my head. Fox said, "No, thank you" and Bill was gone. Peggy half-turned in her chair and squinted at the clock.

"Set begins in fifteen minutes," she said, possibly to

herself. She turned back and smiled at me. "And to think I came home because things were quiet here."

"The flatlanders are ruining the quality of life in the state," Fox said gravely. Peggy laughed.

"My grandmother used to say that people from Massachusetts were a rare piece of work—and she wished they were even rarer." She settled her chin back on her hand. "Anybody know what was in the old station?"

"Drugs," I said.

"Rubies," murmured Fox. "Sables, diamonds, precious manuscripts, and rare perfumes."

Peggy looked at me. "I like his better."

"Me, too," I admitted, and stifled a yawn. "But it's drugs, anyway. I heard Grant McElroy say so."

Peggy nodded absently, then brightened. "Hey! Are you going to be the star witness at the trial? The testimony that puts them all away?"

I stared at her. "God. I hope not."

"And yet you might well be called upon to testify," Fox said. "Perhaps now is the time to hire that lawyer?"

"Perhaps it is, at that," I admitted, around a sinking feeling in my stomach, as Bill returned, bearing a glass of Coke and another beer.

"Thanks," Peggy said, taking the glass and sipping.

"So Mr. Alexander provided Mr. McElroy with drugs and Mr. McElroy provided drugs to greater Wimsy," Fox murmured.

Bill nodded. "That's it, in a nutshell. Another problem being, so a litttle bird told me, that Angel Bolduc recognized Alexander as somebody her brother—the boy who died of an overdose—as somebody her brother used to know, who was involved in his habit. She told Jimmy Danforth about it, of all people . . ."

I took a breath. "And then Angel was killed in a hit-and-run. It wasn't Lisa's death Jimmy was talking about at all."

"No," Bill said seriously, "it wasn't. However, you'll be gratified to learn that the police now believe that Lisa Gagnon was murdered. The theory is that she walked in on McElroy and Alexander while they were doing business."

"And they killed her to keep her quiet," I said, and tried to ignore the image my brain was helpfully providing, of a man holding a terrified woman, shaping her fingers around the gun's grip, holding them there while his accomplice forced her arm up . . .

I gulped air, hand fisting on the table. Fox put his hand over mine, no comment.

Peggy sighed and pushed back her chair. "My set's starting," she said, dropping a hand to Bill's shoulder, and flashing a grin at the rest of us.

"Well." Bill looked at me. "What was it you wanted to discuss, Ms. Pierce? Something about having made a mistake?"

I shook my head. "It's OK. The problem fixed itself."

"I see." He considered me, then had a swallow of beer.

"Reporters," he said, turning his bottle around in his hands. "Good reporters know their towns and their people. They get involved in the heart of the thing, and they care. Caring means that we sometimes make mistakes. But it's better to care than not. Wouldn't you agree, Mr. Foxwell?"

Next to me, Fox started, then inclined his head. "Indeed, Mr. Jacques," he said. "Indeed."

From the front of the room came a ripple of chords, and Peggy stepped up to the mike.

*

We slipped out before the set was done, pleading exhaustion. Peggy waved at us from the tiny stage as we left, stepping out of the Chez's warmth into the frigid night.

I looked up as we walked to our cars; the night sky was

spangled with stars.

"The longest night," Fox murmured. "Are you going to be all right driving home, Jennifer?"

"The car knows the way," I told him, fishing my keys out of my pocket. I stepped toward the Camaro—and turned back.

"Fox," I said, and swallowed. "I'm– I'm invited to a Yule party with the local pagans tomorrow night. Would you– I'd like it, if you would come with me."

He tipped his head in the darkness. "Black tie?"

"Come as you are," I said, feeling a smile on my mouth. "They're good people. I like them."

A small pause, then a soft, "In that case, I'll be pleased to go."

"Good," I said, and smiled, ridiculously happy. "I'll pick you up at eight."

***

About The Author

Best known for her work in the Liaden Universe® with her co-author and husband, Steve Miller, Sharon Lee has been an avid reader of mysteries for most of her life, having been introduced to the Judy Bolton "girl mysteries" at a tender age.

Upon achieving her library card, Sharon immediately located the mystery section at the Carney Branch of the Baltimore County Public Library and in short order consumed the branch's complete holdings of Erle Stanley Gardner, Agatha Christie, Rex Stout, Francis and Richard Lockridge, Dell Shannon, Dashiell Hammet, Raymond Chandler, interspersed with liberal helpings of romantic adventure authors Mary Stewart, Dorothy Eden, and Elswyth Thane, among others.

This combination of early reading matter has had a long-term effect on Sharon's singleton work, and in her collaborative efforts with Steve.

While some of the events in the Jen Pierce novels are reflected in fact, (for instance, in 1988, Sharon and Steve packed up their household and their cats and moved from Baltimore, Maryland to Skowhegan, Maine, where Sharon eventually took a job as newsroom assistant, and then nightside copy editor, at the Morning Sentinel in Waterville. In the meantime, Steve put together **Circular Logic BBS**, at one time the largest computer bulletin board in Central Maine), Jen and Fox lead much more exciting lives than Sharon and Steve do. Which is probably just as well.

In Real Life, Sharon lives just up the road from Wimsy, Maine, with her husband, two cats, lots and lots of books, and a large cast of characters.

With Steve, she is the author of ten science fiction novels and numerous short stories. She is also the author of a dozen single-authored short stories, and two mysteries published by SRM Publisher, Ltd. — *Barnburner* and *Gunshy*. Besides reading, and writing, her interests include seashores, cats, cat whiskers, carousels, and computers. She is a sporadic and not very effective gardener, and, now that the era of community bulletin boards is past, spends 'way too much time playing on the internet.

Visit Sharon Lee on the web at:
http://www.korval.com/liad.htm
or at her Live Journal —
http://rolanni.livejournal.com/

About the Publisher

SRM Publisher Ltd. is an independent press specializing in Science Fiction, Fantasy, and Mystery. With both fiction and non-fiction in the catalog, SRM strives to serve the community of readers, writers, libraries, fans, collectors, and booksellers interested in genre materials.

A direct descendant of **BPLAN Virtuals**, of Waterville, Maine and a more distant descendant of **General Avocations** and **Locust Run Press**, both of Owings Mills, Maryland, SRM was formed in 1995 to publish and distribute what was to be a one shot printing of *Two Tales of Korval*, by Sharon Lee and Steve Miller. Instead, *Two Tales of Korval* went through dozens of printings and sold thousands of copies, serving as a foundation for the chapbooks, trade paper, and hardback books to follow.

SRM Publisher Ltd. now distributes direct through the internet and through genre specialty stores around the world; SRM publications are featured in Books In Print and have been reviewed in **Analog**, **Tangent Online**, **The Morning Sentinel**, and elsewhere.

www.srmpublisher.com